Dedicated to that awful thing known as writer's block.

If it weren't for you this book wouldn't exist.

Meaningful quote here.

THE ART OF DATING

Six months ago, I was naïve, stupid, and whiney.

I believed in second chances.

Even when I was boyfriend-less, apartment less, and my best friend was on me about moving on.

Five months ago, one insignificant moment changed everything.

I met Logan.

I agreed to undergo his ridiculous boot camp to get Cole back.

Last month, a blip in time knocked my world on its axis.

It threw me into free fall without the courtesy of a warning or a safety net.

Yesterday, I ruined everything.

One action that broke two hearts.

I used to believe in second chances.

I had him; I had everything, and i didn't even know it.

My name is Devina Marshal; this is the story of how everything went to shit.

CHAPTER ONE

FIVE MONTHS AGO...

"For the love of everything holy, Devina, stop fidgeting. You look great."

"I look ridiculous," I mumble, not taking my eyes off my reflection. My usual clean face is a sticky, painted mess; dark smoky powder wraps around my brown eyes, my thin lips are coated with thick red paste, and my nonexistent cheekbones sit above false shadows.

"Ridiculously great."

I roll my eyes at her as I attempt, and fail, to pull the red spandex dress lower.

"Stop messing with it and come on. We're going to be late."

"I still fail to see why I'm going," I whine, shrugging into my leather jacket.

THE ART OF DATING

"Ew, you're seriously going to wear that thing?"

"It's February in New York. Yes, I'm wearing this."

She pins me with her best mom-face, "It doesn't match."

"Are we speed dating outside?"

Amy lets out an exasperated sigh before retreating into her closet; reappearing in an attractive grey petticoat that hugs her flawless figure.

"Ready?"

I offer a weak smile and wave towards the door, "After you."

"Ugh, don't be dull. It's going to be fun."

Taking a deep breath, I follow her out of her apartment and out onto the cold New York streets.

"We should have called for a cab rather than trying to hail one down." She complains after a few failed attempts.

"It's only a couple of blocks, why don't we walk?"

"If I weren't wearing Louboutin's, I would."

My eyes fall to her black pumps; they look like ordinary heels to me. I never understood her obsession with expensive brands. Lifting my eyes in time to see a taxi approach the curb.

7

"Wahoo!" She cheers, opening the back door.

Slipping in beside her, I try to swallow the groan when my hand falls into something greasy on the threadbare seat.

"Where to?" The middle-aged driver asks in a thick accent.

"88 Keys on 2nd, please." She tells him before turning her attention to me. "Aren't you just a little bit excited?"

"This isn't my thing, that's all," I confess, watching the traffic crawl through the busy intersection.

"Why not? You're hot and single."

"Barely," I mumble, not wanting to get yet another pep talk.

"You need two things, Devina. A stiff drink and a rebound. Both can be found tonight."

"I need to find an apartment."

"No, what you need to do is kick that sorry son of a bitch out and take back *your* apartment."

"Amy, I've already told you, I don't want the apartment."

"Why? Cause he had little Miss Boob-job there?"

The memory sends a new wave of pain through my chest, six weeks ago I came home to find my longtime boyfriend in bed with my client, they're now living together...in my apartment, while I'm sleeping on my best friend's pull out sofa. "Pretty much."

"You just need a little bleach, that's all." She scoffs and waves nonchalantly watching as the entrance to the bar comes into view.

"Yeah, and a match." I spit back playfully.

"Hopefully he's inside when you do it." She says gathering her purse off the sticky seat. "We're here!" She squeaks enthusiastically. "Let's get you over Cole and under someone new."

CHAPTER TWO

The piano bar is relatively crowded as we enter, tables are arranged in neat little rows, housing two chairs each. Amy pulls me over to a fold-out table near the entrance where we each receive a numbered sticker and a clipboard. The woman issuing us our items explains that we will start at one end and work our way down. We will have two minutes to mingle with each man before moving to the next participant. If we want to further the conversation we mark the table on our clipboard, this is the point I stop paying attention; I'm only here to humor Ames, she lives for this kind of thing, me on the other hand? I'd prefer to be in comfortable clothing, lounging in front of my T.V while eating myself into a coma. After the woman finishes talking, Amy goes to order us drinks, instructing me to get in line.

Every couple of minutes a small buzzer goes off near the bar, and the rotation moves. There's a broader variety of people than I had expected; some women are dressed up like Amy and myself where others are dressed casually like I wanted to. One girl is even walking around in red plaid pajama pants and a white tank top that's tied behind her back. The men are equally as diverse, though it's hard to get a decent look at their faces seeing as most of them are hidden behind the heads of the female attendees.

My nerves have reached DEFCON 1 by the time Amy returns with two mojitos and a shot glass.

"Here, down this." She hands me the small glass filled with what I assume is tequila.

"Liquid courage, right?" I shrug, tipping the glass back. Warmth spreads through my body immediately.

"I'll take that; you take this." She takes the empty glass from my hands, replacing it with a mojito before turning back to the bar.

I squeeze the lime and mix the mint leaves around while I anxiously await her return.

"Do you want to go first?" She teases, stepping in front of me, knowing my answer already.

"Absolutely, not."

"Deal. I can talk you up before you get there." Her serious expression breaks at the sight of my face, struggling to keep herself from laughing, she continues. "You know, warm them up." She takes a sip of her drink to hide her smile.

"Make sure to tell them I love hookers and cocaine, that's always a good conversation starter."

"Oh, of course." She nods.

"But not just any cocaine, the super expensive kind."

"And expensive hookers, right?"

"No, no. Just regular hookers. I gotta save up my money for the good cocaine."

"Ah, yes. How silly of me."

We both smile and my mood begins to lift. That feeling soon fades as the buzzer sounds, sending Amy to sit down at the first table. She moves so gracefully, so calculated. She's like a Venus flytrap, knowing exactly how to lure them in. I watch her perfectly timed laughs and seemingly innocent touches lock this poor guy in. She's an amazing friend and a genuinely good person, but she gets bored easily and blames romance movies for having such high expectations. She knows as well as I do that any guy she takes home with her tonight probably won't make it to a second date. Pulling the sleeve of my coat into my palm, I nervously ball the fabric while the time dwindles down. All too quickly the bell rings.

I sit awkwardly in front of Mr. 0271 after Amy pretends to shoot herself over his shoulder.

"Guess how old I am." He demands with no introductions.

"I don't know."

"Come on, guess!" He jumps in excitement.

I aim low, "27?"

"Nope. Try again."

"Seriously?" He nods, "Um, 29?"

"Nope, lower."

"28?"

He let out an obnoxious laugh and shakes his head, clearly happy about his game.

"Has anyone guessed correctly yet?"

He shakes his head still wearing his weird smile; it looks painful.

"But I'm really good at guessing women's ages. You're..." he rubs his chin as he stares at me. "36."

"Wow." He's about nine years off there. "Incredible."

"I know."

The bell rings, releasing me. This is horrendous. Amy quickly moves up without a second look behind her, so maybe this guy is some semblance of normal. Removing my jacket, I sit down with Mr. 0346.

"Hello. I'm Devina."

"Alex." He mumbles, still looking at his folded hands in his lap.

Folding my lips in, I take a look around the room waiting for him to speak. When he doesn't, I take a deep breath and try to break the awkward silence, "How are you?"

"Good."

"Are you enjoying your night?"

"Sure."

"Oh, kay."

I'm all out of small talk at this point, so I end up watching the ice float in my drink until the bell rings. "It was nice meeting you, Alex."

I stand up and find Amy still talking with the next suitor; maybe she found herself a man. As I stand over her shoulder, he glances up, and our eyes meet. He's attractive; dark hair is styled neatly, showing off his light eyes under a thick fan of lashes. No wonder Amy's still pawing over him, especially after the first two tables.

Pulling his blue eyes off me, he looks back at her and nods in my direction causing Amy to twist to see what he's nodding at. She lets out a girlish giggle and shakes his hand.

Once vacating the seat, she passes his shoulder and spins around fanning herself. I give her a small smile before moving to take my seat.

"Logan Devitt." He holds out his hand.

I shake his outstretched hand and sit. "Devina Anderson."

"What do you do, Devina?" Oh good, normal conversation.

"I do freelance publishing."

"What is that?"

"I'm an independent contractor; I edit novels for self-publishers."

"Do you enjoy it?"

"Most of the time. What about you? What do you do?"

"I'm an entrepreneur focusing primarily on telecommunication networking and mobile marketing. I make roughly six million a year."

Yeah right and I'm Arnold Schwarzenegger.

THE ART OF DATING

"Impressive. Do you often win the affection of ladies by stating the bottom line of your bank account?"

I just wanted a normal conversation. Is that so hard to ask? I've had weird guess-my-age guy, awkward silent guy, and now pathological liar guy.

He lets out a small chuckle, leaning forward to rest his stubbled chin on his closed fist.

"I wouldn't use the term 'win,' but yes, stating my wealth usually gets me the date."

I nod my head unimpressed.

"But not you?"

"No, not me," I state plainly.

He smiles and runs his finger across his bottom lip; if he wasn't so arrogant, I might find him attractive.

"What about dinner in Italy?"A scoff escapes my lips before I have time to put my emotions in check. "Not a fan? Alright, Paris then?"

I shake my head, unable to think of a proper response. His smile grows while his eyes narrow as if he's trying to figure me out. I suppose other girls throw themselves at him, believing he's some millionaire. Yeah right, a millionaire in a four-star bar in East Village, New York, at a speed-dating event nonetheless? Ridiculous.

Thankfully, the buzzer frees me from his gaze. I grab my coat and stand before he stops me. "You never answered my question."

"What question?"

"Dinner in Paris."

"As generous as your offer is, my affections are not for sale."

With that, I turn on my heels and walk away. Caught up in my thoughts I walk right past the next suitor. Refusing to embarrass myself and turn around, I head to the bar and order another drink. The audacity of some people, I swear.

CHAPTER THREE

I make it through half my drink before Amy sits down beside me. "What happened?"

"This is ridiculous."

"There's that word again, *ridiculous*."

"Well, it is. The first guy was all 'Guess my age, Guess my age,' the second was too shy to speak to me, and the third guy was telling this elaborate story about being a millionaire, it's just too much." I shake my head while chipping the polish off my nails.

"The first two were ridiculous as you put it, but that third guy was hot."

I roll my eyes and go back to picking at the teal remains around my cuticles. I'd rather be curled up on the couch watching some mindless television with Cole right now. Too bad his dick was buried in little miss Monica Claire.

"He was! And what if he *is* a millionaire?" She looks smitten.

"Oh, my best friend, the gold digger."

"I am not!" She playfully slaps my arm, glancing in his direction. "You think he was lying?"

Yes, though I know if I say that she'll argue. "You have your phone, don't you?"

"Yeah, you don't have yours?"

"No, I left it at your apartment. Google him."

A huge smile spreads across her face before she opens her clutch purse, fishing out her iPhone.

"Siri, Google 'Logan Devitt, New York."

Amy curses under her breath when her phone looks up Logan debit rather than Logan Devitt.

"What's the point of having a smartphone if it isn't smart?" She complains, fixing the error in the search bar. "Okay, here we go."

She stares at the little screen before smiling a brilliant in-your-face-Anderson smile, showing me the screen before reading out loud, "New York Times reported two months ago about the 1.6 million dollar donation from Mr. Logan

Devitt to the American Children's Cancer Association. It looks like his family is also wealthy; his parents, Jonathan and Caroline Devitt, donated as well." Her fingers move like bullets across the screen as she researches him further. "Oh, wow. His parents have multiple foundations too."

"He could share the same name."

"Devitt isn't exactly a popular name, Dee."

"He could be pretending to be this guy."

"Why are you so argumentative?" She laughs, still typing away on her phone.

"Why would a millionaire be in a piano bar speed dating?"

"I don't know; maybe he's a human being like the rest of us?" She gasps in horror.

"He's not the real guy, I'm telling you."

She smirks, shaking her head. We fall into silence, her on her phone while I'm stuck in my head thinking about Cole and the five years we were together.

"Ha!" Amy yells, making me jump. "Look!"

She twists her phone, showing a google image search, the same guy as before stands at multiple organizations and events.

"He's a millionaire!"

"Millionaire or not, he's still arrogant."

"How was he arrogant?"

"His tone, him offering to whisk a girl to Italy, or Paris for dinner."

I glance her way when she fails to respond; her mouth is open and twisted, she looks almost jealous.

"He offered to take you to *Paris*?"

"No, not exactly. I think he was just trying to sound impressive."

"What did you say?" She scoots her bar stool closer to me as if it's top secret information.

"I said no."

"What? Why the hell would you do that?"

Her horror is enough to make me laugh."Because I didn't believe him. Besides, why would I want to be trapped in another country with someone I spent literally two minutes with?"

"Because he's a millionaire!"

"He's arrogant."

"Do you know what that word means?"

"No, I'm just using it to sound cool." I deadpan, "Yes, I know what it means."

"Okay, well, I don't think he has an inflated ego."

"Thinking he can have whoever he wants just because of his bank account makes him arrogant."

"Ugh," She groans, "Find another word to use."

"Vain, smug, pretentious, take your pick."

"You should have said yes. I'm sure the paparazzi would have taken your picture and made Cole eat his heart out."

"The paparazzi? He said he does something with phones, not star in movies."

"The paparazzi followed Christian and Ana." She's so adorable staring at me like that proves her point.

"That's a book, Ames. Not real life."

"So? I bet he has a red room like Christian Grey."

"Why don't you go find out?"

"Honey, if he circled my number you bet your sweet little ass I will."

Laughing, I stare at my drink. I hope this night ends quickly; I have a ton of work to do to make up losing Monica Claire as a client.

"Seeing as he's staring at you, you might have to find out for me."

"He is not," I look over my shoulder just to lock eyes with said millionaire. I quickly turn back around wide-eyed, "He's probably looking at the bar."

Amy smirks, adjusting herself on the bar stool, "He's coming over."

"No, he's not." I gape at her, fighting the urge to look for myself.

Her flirtatious smile makes its appearance as she plays with her straw, "Mr. Devitt."

The stool to my left moves as I feel him sit down beside me, "You didn't go to the next table. Can I assume it's because you found what you were looking for?"

"I found the pool of men lackluster," I smile sweetly at him.

"Ouch." His smile curves to the right, "Perhaps we should request more than two minutes."

I laugh, "Two minutes was plenty."

"Apparently not if you found me lackluster."

"No amount of time is going to redeem that."

He smiles, "I'm certain I could change your mind."

"Doubtful." Pulling my coat off my lap, I stand, catching Amy's glare. "I'm catching a cab home."

Her face turns to disappointment.

"Why don't you practice your charm on Amy?" I smile at each in turn, stepping away from the bar.

With a small wave to Amy, I retreat outside deciding to walk rather than pay for a cab. Sure, it would be faster to take a taxi, but funds are a little tight at the moment, and now I need to mentally prepare for the wrath of Ames when she gets home. With any luck, she'll go home with Mr. Money Bags and all will be forgiven.

CHAPTER FOUR

All was not forgiven. Amy came home angrier than a hornet, giving me her two cents about my wallowing, I knew she was furious when she didn't sugarcoat anything. Telling me she understands being a man-hater at the moment, but leaving her at the bar was breaking every girl code in the handbook. Even though nine out of ten times, I'm abandoned when she disappears with a guy, however I decided it was in my best interest not to point that out.

She tried to stay angry at me, but once she said her peace she cracked. After plopping down on the couch next to me, I was fed every detail of what happened after I left. I'm positive she was stretching the truth, claiming, 'The

25

Millionaire' as he has been named, wouldn't stop talking about me. Where in truth, I'm sure he asked maybe two questions then left. She also claimed to pass him up because, 'that's what friends do,' and I had staked a claim. How she got leaving as staking a claim is beyond me.

Thankfully, throughout the week the topic of Logan Devitt died, being replaced with excitement of Mardi Gras parties next week; I will absolutely be getting out of that. I have zero interest in bar-hopping in New York City while Amy hooks up with countless guys, I love her to death, but that just isn't my bag.

Finishing three manuscripts, I find myself breathing easier knowing I can finally start looking into apartments. Hopefully outside of East Village and nowhere near Lenox Hill to avoid running into my ex, though, now that I think of it, it might be nice to rub it in his face when I bring guys over...or look like a total loser when I don't. I mentally cross Lenox Hill off the list.

"What are you up to?" Amy walks out of her bedroom looking like she just climbed out of a magazine.

"Looking at apartments."

"Dee, just go get *your* apartment back."

"I. Don't. Want. It." I say slowly, hoping this time it'll sink in.

She rolls her eyes as she walks into the kitchen, looking out of place as usual. She was created for luxury, everything about her screams wealth even though she lives in a tiny one-bedroom apartment, using her fashion degree as a personal shopper in some ritzy shop in Manhattan.

In the fifth grade, we made a pact to move here believing all the glamorous lies the television told us. Nothing had prepared us for the price tag of New York City when we escaped Boston; we'd both rather make just enough to survive than admit defeat and move back home; even if we'd both be better off there.

"What about Tribeca?" I ask, looking at a listing for a one bedroom apartment in a former industrial building.

She makes a face, "That's where all the hipsters are."

"Okay, Yorkville?"

"Hmm, maybe if you can find an affordable one. Oh! See if there are any on 5th Ave."

"Yeah, right. I couldn't afford 5th Ave in my wildest dreams, at least not one facing Central Park."

THE ART OF DATING

"You're probably right, but let's look anyway."

Tossing herself down on the cushion beside me, she lays her head on my shoulder watching as I change my search. Of course, there are listings that make us drool, the apartments you see in the movies, the ones we were convinced we'd live in together as children.

After we blew the better part of the morning running through listing ads that we could never afford, Ames left for work while I wrote down a few promising addresses only to find them to be a bust, one had promise but I'd have to average six clients a month just to cover rent, not including all the additional nonsense like food and electricity, they'll pay for your cable though. I mentally roll my eyes, maybe I should kick Cole out, I mean it is my apartment, and he would deserve it. I know I won't do it though, I seem to have this theory that he'll come back begging for my forgiveness, if I kick him out that'll never happen. Which is reason number eight hundred and twenty-seven why Amy insists I go out and 'get under someone new.' In her opinion, I'm holding onto false hope that Cole will 'grow up and stop being an asshole.' She just doesn't know him like I do. Seeing as they never really got along, I don't think she had the opportunity to get to know him the way I do. Cole did so many sweet things like kissing me goodbye, always making sure the door was locked, and he always kept me updated with his plans. Sure, they're small, but the small things add up. Truth is; yes, Cole was wrong. Yes, he broke my heart. But people make mistakes, and I can't rationalize throwing away a five-year relationship over one mistake.

CHAPTER FIVE

Arriving home Saturday night I immediately know this evening is doomed. Amy has two garment bags hanging from her bedroom door, meaning my plan of binge-watching Netflix has been officially booted.

Slowly moving back, my fingers wrap around the knob.

"About time." She yells from her bedroom.

Damnit. There goes any thoughts of sneaking back out.

"I told you I didn't want to go out." I groan, throwing my purse onto her kitchen island that works more like a shelf than a place to eat.

"It's Mardi Gras. We've been talking about this all week."

"No, you've been talking about it all week, I've had a date planned with your television."

"I rented us costumes; we're going."

Stopping mid-step, I gawk at her bedroom, "You rented costumes?"

"Yeah, the bar down the street is offering free drinks to those who come in dressed up."

"It's not Halloween."

"No shit, Sherlock." She says finally emerging from the bedroom to unzip the first bag.

I stare in horror, taking in the tiny green sequin dress."That better be yours,"

"Wait until you see the mask!" She fishes out this ugly thing with fake flowers and feathers covering the side.

"I'm not wearing that."

"The shoes are the best part though," She hoists a pair of purple heels with peacock feathers up the center.

"Fuck no."

Laughter erupts from her lungs, "Your face!"

"It's not funny."

She blows out a deep breath, putting the mask and shoes back into the bag, "It really is but to keep your heart from failing, no, that's my costume."

31

My stomach churns, "I'm scared to see your runner-up option."

"Oh, hush. It is not my runner-up." I quirk my brow at her, "I wouldn't wear yours." Her smile turns mischievous.

Oh, no. God, have mercy.

She unzips the second bag revealing another tiny scrap of fabric. It's a deep purple with some sort of rhinestone design on the bodice.

"It's not awful," I admit, "I'm still going to freeze my ass off in it though."

Seemingly unimpressed with my lack of enthusiasm she levels me with a glare, "Well, they were all out of yoga pants and oversized ex-boyfriend sweaters."

"Good thing I already have a pair." I tug on Cole's Yankees hoodie.

She huffs, reaching for the bottom of the bag.

Removing a purple mask with green and gold designs and a pair of green heels with more straps than a cargo ship, she points at me with a manicured finger, "Don't. You're going, and you're wearing this outfit."

I sigh, "How about I wear the mask with jeans and a nice jacket."

"No! You're twenty-seven, not forty. Stop trying to hide how hot you are and wear the damn dress."

"Ames. It's twelve degrees outside."

"You won't even feel it after you get a couple of shots in you."

"I should be allowed to dress myself seeing as you dolled me up last weekend. It's only fair."

"No."

"Why?" I whine.

"Because no one's going to buy you drinks if you show up looking like a soccer mom and we both know we can't afford to buy our own drinks. Especially after I used our rent money to rent these outfits."

"You used rent money? Ames!" I scold, rubbing my forehead. She's delusional if she thinks her parents can continue pulling her ass out of the fires she creates.

"What? This month is covered, and I can swing nexts. Don't worry." Before I can contest it, she continues with her best guilt-whine, "We barely got to hang out when you were with Cole. Bastard always kept you locked away."

"He did not. I don't like partying; you know that."

"Not always, but you occasionally do."

33

"Occasionally being the key word here."

Her eyes narrow further before her face relaxes, "Please? I'll stop forcing you to go out if you come. I won't even make you dance with anyone. You can be a hermit in the corner for all I care, but you're going to look pretty when you do it."

"Promise?"

A delighted smile blesses her pouted lips, "On our friendship. Now get dressed."

With a satisfied smile, she throws the dress, hanger and all, at me. Catching it in midair, I groan.

God, if you're listening, tonight would be a good time to introduce her to her soulmate or maybe lower her alcohol tolerance. I'm fine with either.

CHAPTER SIX

An hour later, we're entering the bar offering free drinks.

People are everywhere, and I'm glad we're not the only ones dressed up. Some look like they just came from a masquerade ball.

"Bottoms up," Amy tells me clinking her shot glass to mine.

Whatever I just drank definitely isn't from their top shelf, Amy and I cringe at the bitter sting.

With the obscene amount of people and the alcohol coursing through my veins, I'm surprisingly warm in the little bar. Following Amy, she leads me through the crowd, finding a table near the back. From here I'm able to get a look around. Red and orange bulbs line the walls leading to a small stage; open mic night comes to mind.

"We need to find guys," Amy says, craning her neck to get a better look.

"Or, I'll cash in my free drinks, and then we can go get some food."

"We just got here." She scolds.

Amy has the ability to go an entire day without eating, I, on the other hand, invented the term 'hangry' and it looks a lot like Godzilla on its period with poison ivy up its ass.

"You should cash in for your free shots though; I don't know how long they're handing them out."

Taking out my I.D, I hand her my bag for safe keeping before weaseling my way through the crowd. Once at the bar, I get up on my tiptoes, resting my weight on my forearms and wait for the bartender to notice me.

The noise of everyone's conversations around me is deafening. The bartender, who turns out to be super cute finally turns around, baby blue eyes find mine, and I raise my hand to wave my card at him. Tall, blonde, and gorgeous stands in front of me ready to take my order.

Lifting the flyer off the table, I point to the section about free drinks. He holds up his hand

36

before tapping the back of it, I show him mine, and he produces a stamp and pad before marking my hand in black ink. I admire his face while he pours, if it weren't so loud in here, I'd imagine he'd have one of those sexy Georgian accents.

Two shots of swine later, I'm pushing my way back to Amy when I notice she's no longer at our table. With the heavy base of the music I can't hear it, but I feel the vibration of my groan as I look around for her. I hate when she does this, never one to pass up an opportunity with a cute guy.

After scouring the dance floor, I finally spot her grinding against some guy in one of those creepy masks with the long nose. She smiles sweetly at my glare when I reach her, accepting one of the glasses. Her dancing partner stands patiently behind her while we down our free drinks, handing me her empty glass after she swallows, along with my bag.

"When do you want to move to the next bar? Preferably one with food." I yell, leaning into her shoulder.

She shrugs, stepping back into her new boy-toy's space. She holds up two fingers signaling two more songs. I nod and move to the side of the stage to wait. I feel like a creep while lurking in the shadows but it's better than getting shoulder checked every five seconds.

Amy's my favorite person in the world, but I've never understood the hype about bars and dancing with strangers when you can be drinking in a steakhouse with a massive chunk of meat instead.

Two songs turn into seven before she comes over to tell me she's ready to go.

Making a quick escape, we walk arm in arm down the sidewalk until the next bar comes into view.

"Ames." I groan, "I haven't eaten since yesterday, I'm starving."

"I'm sure they have something inside."

"Peanuts don't count."

She smirks, "One drink, two songs, and then we'll find somewhere with a kitchen, deal?"

I nod and follow behind her. Little did I know, she meant one drink that someone else pays for. We've been here for over an hour, and I'm starting to get stabby.

"Hey." She yells approaching; her face flushed, the overhead light reflecting off the sweat misting at her hairline.

"Ready?"

"Actually," She draws out, folding her lips in, "I kinda met this wicked hot guy, and I was thinking about-"

"Go." I interrupt her, "Have fun."

"What are you going to do?"

"I'm going to find a diner, and then I'll catch a cab home."

"You sure you don't mind?"

"Nope, go."

An excited smile lights up her face as she pulls me into a hug, "I love you!"

Twisting around, she disappears into the crowd. Most people would be upset if their best friend deserted them, not me though. My prayers have been answered; now I can get food, change into comfortable clothes and practice the art of being a potato in front of the T.V like I've wanted to do all day; I call this a win.

Stepping outside, I dump my mask into my purse before wrapping my arms around my waist trying to stay warm while searching for a diner.

"Hey!" I hear someone call behind me, but I keep walking. "Wait up."

Footsteps start to close in as my heart picks up pace, glancing behind me I see a figure

39

dressed in all black, wearing a mask that covers over half his face, "Hey, you're the girl from that piano bar, aren't you?"

I try to ignore the cloaked figure, but my pulse is reaching an all-time high.

"You and your friend were at the speed dating at 88 Keys."

Reason number four hundred and eighty-two why that was a bad idea, that bar was full of people.

"I think you have me confused with someone else." I try to sound confident, but my voice betrays me.

"It's a-" he runs ahead of me cutting me off. My heart is going to beat right out of my chest. An entrance door down the street opens as two masked guests leave for the evening. I step around him abruptly cutting off his train of thought and walk towards the couple, at least there will be witnesses. "Devina, right?"

My stride falters a moment at the sound of my name. How the hell does this person know my name? Oye, that's too creepy for words.

"I have to get going," I say over my shoulder. My pace speeds up when I hear the sound of approaching feet, he's following me.

Should I scream? I mean, he hasn't actually done anything, but he looks like how I imagine

Jack the Ripper would have looked, and it's unsettling.

"Are your affections still off the market?"

This makes me stop. I turn slowly to face my hooded stranger.

"You're that guy." I hiss, angrier than I had intended. "That arrogant jerk who thought he could woo all the ladies by offering extravagant European trips or whatever."

"Whoa, arrogant?" He laughs, proving my arrogant theory. "Because I offered to take you to Paris? You seem to have a shallow opinion of me. What's more shocking is the fact that your opinion is so low when we've yet to have a real conversation."

"Attempting to buy my affection and then stalking me at night like a masked serial killer isn't exactly winning you any favors."

He laughs, untying his mask. "Better?"

"A little." He's prettier than I remember and I kind of wish he'd put it back on. "Why are you following me?"

"I recognized your friend; she told me you were leaving so I was trying to catch up with you."

"That doesn't answer my question."

"I wanted to ask you to dinner."

"No, thanks."

41

"Why not? Isn't that where you were headed?"

"How did you-" The question dies in my throat when I realize if he ran into Amy she would have squealed like a pig.

"Your friend told me." I nod along, having already figured that part out. "So how about it?"

"Gonna have to pass."

Hiking up my purse I start forward once again.

"What if I let you pay for your own meal?"

"Still a no," I call over my shoulder, leaving him in the shadows behind me.

My adrenaline is racing from when I thought he was going to mug me; I can feel my knees wobble with each step. No matter, the streets get busier in a couple of blocks- a small scream escapes my lips when a loud clatter rings out from the alley to my right.

I spin to face my certain death when a cat scrambles across my feet; its panicked claws tearing across exposed skin as it tries escaping the aluminum lid that's still spinning on its side.

"Logan!" I turn, hoping he's still on the street somewhere.

Rubbing my forehead, I try to steady my breathing as his hooded frame turns around, "Sure."

I hike my shoulders up in a nonchalant shrug even though my nerves are shot, my skin is clammy, and my pulse beats frantically against my neck.

"Yeah?" He doesn't move towards me, so I walk briskly back in his direction.

"Yeah, why not?"

The corner of his mouth tips up, "Where to?"

CHAPTER SEVEN

Thanks to the cat who clawed my feet to shit I'm able to focus on the sting of my flesh rather than the uncomfortable silence of the diner.

A plump woman in a red apron ushers us to an empty booth before scurrying off the way we came. Logan stands while I slide into the worn leather bench before taking a seat on the opposite side.

Scooping the menu off the rack, I flip it open ready to order everything in sight.

"What does one order from an establishment such as this?"

I don't raise my head from the menu as I answer. "Food."

"Very good." He chuckles, plucking a menu for himself. "Anything you recommend?"

"Never been here before."

Our waitress returns, running her hands over the pockets of her apron before grabbing her pad.

"What can I get you?"

"I'll have the double diner burger with everything, loaded french fries, a chocolate shake and a coke, please."

She nods, turning to Logan who's busy staring at me, a small smile begins to form on his lips, "I'll have the same."

Turning on her heels, she quietly retreats as I take his menu and place is back on the rack.

"That's a lot of food."

"With any luck it will be."

My fingers tap against the sticky surface of the table while my eyes wander around the bare establishment. Everything is themed to have that 1950's feel with large classic car prints, checkered flooring, and red upholstery. They even have one of those countertop jukeboxes on the counter of the wrap around bar.

"You look festive tonight."

I don't know why I glance down at my dress; I know what I'm wearing. Still, my eyes travel over the rhinestone bodice and flowing skirt. Raising my head I offer a tight-lipped smile; I look like a joke. "It was Amy's idea. They were offering free drinks at one of the bars to anyone who dressed up. I'm surprised you noticed her in that mask."

He chuckles lightly, "Well when she came barreling into the men's restroom with her date, I have to admit it took me a moment to place her."

I hide my snort under my palm, "I'm sorry you had to see that."

"It was quite comical, actually. I've never been witness to something like that before."

"Hang out with her long enough; nothing will surprise you," I say, pulling back to give the waitress room to set our drinks down.

Placing my straw into my shake, I take a long pull.

"Your order will be up shortly."

"Thank you." Logan smiles, delicately unwrapping his straw.

"You look out of place," I observe.

"How so?"

"Well, the way you're sitting for one, all straight-backed and constipated." He cracks a smile, letting his shoulders sag half an inch,

"And you're undressing your straw like you plan on keeping the wrapper."

"And how does one properly unwrap a plastic straw?"

Collecting my secondary straw, I pinch the center and pull, separating the paper in two before dunking it into my cola. "Like that."

His smile grows, "I hadn't realized there was proper straw etiquette. You have my sincerest apologies."

I bow my head, "Apology accepted."

He chuckles, and I loathe the fact I enjoy the deep tone of it so much. Perhaps Amy's right, maybe I've just been in a man-hating mood, Logan's not so bad.

"So, what are you doing out in East Village?"

"What if I live here?"

"We both know you don't. If you did, you'd know how to open a straw. I'd guess you live in the Upper East Side."

He smiles with amusement, "You're not wrong."

"I know." That's where all the rich people live, "So what pulled you to East Village not one but two weekends in a row?"

"I enjoy the nightlife here; it's an entirely different world from what I'm used to."

47

"Champagne and tuxedos get boring for you?"

"Bourbon is more my style."

"Yeah, I'm sure it's real rough living on the top of the world like that." I smile to let him know I'm only kidding.

"Well, the air is thinner up there." He shrugs which seems so out of place with his rich-bitch haircut and a well-trimmed beard. "Sometimes it's nice to slip down here and fill my lungs."

"Playboy millionaire who enjoys speed dating and bar hopping." I quirk an eyebrow, "I smell rebellion against the family business. Do you enjoy crashing your car and tabloid scandals?"

"Only on Sundays."

I laugh, "Sundays are when I like to get blind drunk and beat Amy."

"Ah, see." He points at me, "We all have our outlets."

My smile remains in place as the waitress sets our plates down. It smells divine. You know when you're about to eat a damn good burger when grease visibly seeps out of your patty.

"Are you going to be able to finish that?"

"Yup." Spinning my plate in a circle, I admire the feast I'm about to consume as I speak, "Might even eat yours if you take too long."

He chuckles like I'm kidding. With a shrug, I pick up my enormous burger, taking a very impolite bite. Oh, this is heaven! I'm still chewing when I force another massive bite, finding room for two fries while I'm at it.

I nearly spit across the table when an involuntary laugh takes ahold of me. Logan is perched in front of me, cutting his burger into pieces with utensils looking like the Queen of England.

"What the hell are you doing?" I say around my mouthful. "It's a burger, not some fancy steak, pick it up and eat it."

Washing the half-chewed food down with my coke, I continue to stare in disbelief.

"I have facial hair." He says by way of explanation.

I laugh, "And?"

"Do you know how hard it is to wash the grease out? I have no plans of smelling like a slaughterhouse for the duration of my evening."

I chuckle again, shoving my face into my food. I have no such reservations. If I smell like a slaughterhouse, I'll just remember how amazing this food was.

THE ART OF DATING

Cleaning my plate in record time, I set it on the edge of the table to be picked up, drawing the remains of my shake in front of me while Logan continues with his half-eaten plate.

"Were we racing?" He asks, eyeing my plate.

"Nope." Reaching forward, I steal one of his fries and dunk it into my shake.

He chuckles, pushing his plate forward, "I'm impressed."

"You should see me at a buffet, now that's impressive."

"You're telling me you're capable of eating more?"

"I could finish your plate and still have room for pie." Oh, pie.

Grabbing the menu, I flip it over to the dessert section.

"I know grown men who can't eat that much."

"And that's why I'm your most impressive friend." Blueberry or Cherry, they both sound divine.

"Oh, so we're friends now?"

"Sure." Raising my hand, I grab our waitress' attention.

"I thought I was, 'that arrogant guy.'"

"Yeah, well, you've been upgraded. Can I get a slice of blueberry pie?" I ask the waitress who nods and disappears.

"What instigated the promotion?"

"I find you amusing."

"How so?"

"You cut your burger into little bite-sized pieces," I shrug.

He laughs outright, "What will it take to get a second date?"

"A first would be helpful."

He smiles, and I catch my mistake. That was meant to imply we weren't on a date, not an invitation to ask. "Go to dinner with me."

"No, thank you."

He deflates lightheartedly, "Why not?"

"Because I'm spoken for."

"Is that right?"

"Yes." I jut out my chin.

"You forget we met at a speed dating event."

"I was dragged there by Amy."

"Where was this significant other tonight?"

Probably six inches deep in little Miss Author. "We're..."

"Lies aren't kind."

"I never lie," I state in defense.

"Everyone lies."

"Not me. I simply reword things to be less harsh, but I never lie."

He squares his shoulders in challenge, "Are you currently in a relationship?"

"Yes and no, it's difficult to answer that."

"Explain it then."

"We never formally broke up."

"Ah." He purses his lips to cover his smile. "So he walked out."

"No." I glare, "I was the one who left."

He holds his reply until the waitress drops the plate in front of me.

"If you were the one to leave, I'm confused how you would still be in a relationship."

"Cole made a mistake. I'm waiting for him to come to his senses and apologize."

"What was the mistake?"

"None of your business."

"Dodging and lying go hand in hand you know."

"I'm not dodging. His discretions aren't up for public conversation."

"Are you suggesting we move this to a less public area?" He asks with a wolfish grin. "Say, my place?"

"Absolutely not," I answer in horror.

"I hear revenge is sweet." He quips, wiping the table with his napkin.

"Revenge is poison."

He shrugs, "Merely making a suggestion."

"I won't throw away a five-year relationship just to get even."

"So he cheated." It's not a question.

"What makes you think that?"

"Your choice of words. You said to get even, not revenge."

"It's none of your business."

"Was it because you're boring?"

Defensive anger builds in my stomach, "I'm not boring."

"If you aren't, why was he looking?"

"He wasn't 'looking,' it just happened."

He laughs as my anger starts to boil over, "Honey, that's always the excuse."

"How would you know?" I seethe, standing up.

Thankfully my anger is enough to numb the scorching pain of my thighs. Fairly certain I left a layer of skin back on the booth seat. God, i hate dresses.

Marching up to the counter, I wave a twenty at the waitress and lay it on the bar counter before storming out of the restaurant.

The chill of the night assaults my face as I exit, stepping off the ledge I try to put as much distance between me and that asshole as I can before the bell above the door sounds.

"What if I could help you get him back?"

My stride falters at his words.

Slowly I turn to face him, "And why would you do that?"

"You said it yourself; we're friends."

I scoff, "Friends don't ask what you did to cause someone else to cheat."

He closes the gap between us as he speaks, "Everything I've heard leads me to believe he isn't worth the time, with that being said, I'm still willing to help you get him back."

"And how would you be able to do that?"

"Simple, I teach you how to master the art of dating."

"The art of dating? Yeah right, that's not even a thing."

"The art of dating is where you trick someone into dating you without them knowing. You dangle something they can't have right in front of their face and watch as they fall unknowingly into your web."

"And how do you plan on dangling me in front of his face? He knows he can have me."

"Which is why we take you off the market, make him question it."

"What, like a pretend relationship?"

"No, that would be lying. The art is to manipulate the situation, make him perceive an innocent event into something much bigger. Allow his mind to become his enemy."

"He knows me too well; he'd never believe I'd move on."

"That's why we're going to remake you."

My head automatically pulls back, "Remake me?"

He nods once, "I'm going to make you the ultimate prize. He'll be crawling back on his hands and knees before your birthday."

"You're going to accomplish this before May?"

"Before my birthday." He smiles, easing some of my tension.

"He'll never buy it. You haven't seen the girl he's with."

"No, but I've seen you."

I roll my eyes, "He'll never go for it."

"A bet then?"

"No way. I'm not betting my relationship."

"Just hear me out." He groans like I'm the most difficult person he's ever talked to."If he isn't crawling back by Thanksgiving, you have to go on a date with me."

"I'm not betting."

"When he comes crawling back, all you have to do is buy me dinner."

"I'm. Not. Betting."

"Wuss." He smiles.

"I am not a wuss."

"Sure about that? You're kind of acting like one, big time."

"Logan."

"Prove you're not a wuss, then. Accept the bet."

I growl, looking down the street, catching the attention of a cab. I hate being challenged, "Fine. Whatever, deal."

A triumphant smile seals the deal, "May I see your phone?"

"Why?"

"To exchange phone numbers."

Slowly, I offer my phone forward.

After he enters his information he accesses the dial pad, a moment later an audible vibration escapes his pocket.

"Well, Miss Anderson. It was a pleasure."

"You remember my last name?"

The corner of his lip raises once again, "You remembered mine. Enjoy the rest of your evening."

"Wait," I freeze, clasping the chilly yellow door handle, "Do you want to share a cab?"

"That won't be necessary." As if on cue, a shiny black car approaches the curb. "Goodnight, Devina."

I give him a tight-lipped smile before climbing into the cab feeling like this could go really well or very, very poorly.

CHAPTER EIGHT

Thankfully, I arrived home before Amy and was able to avoid her onslaught of questions by pretending to be asleep when she came stumbling in. Also thankful when she spent all of yesterday nursing her hangover, and had very little to say other than an occasional grunt or vow to never drink again.

As I conclude another chapter of the manuscript I'm editing, I say a silent prayer that she stays asleep until the last available moment before rushing to get ready for work. I don't think she'd judge me necessarily, but I do believe she'll blow this arrangement with Logan entirely out of proportion, and I don't need any more reason to back down.

THE ART OF DATING

I've been debating canceling on and off since I received his text this morning instructing me to arrive at an attached address today at one. It's nearing half past eleven, and I still haven't made up my mind.

If he can do what he claims, then I win. But, if he doesn't, I look like a stage five clinger who can't take a hint that her ex-boyfriend doesn't want her. That or he could be some murderer, and this whole thing could turn Hannibal Lecter real fast. Speaking of that, I need to pick up lotion today.

Pulling a notebook off the coffee table, I rip a piece of paper out and quickly jot down some things we need.

"Hey." I jump at Amy's gravelly voice.

"Gah, you scared me."

"Sorry." She smiles, scrubbing the side of her head with her acrylic nails.

"I'm going to run to the store and pick some stuff up. Need anything?"

"A higher alcohol tolerance. I still feel like shit."

"Alright, but only if it's on clearance."

She smiles, turning on the coffee machine. "I'm going to go take a shower, you gonna be here when I get out?"

"Probably not. I'm going to finish this chapter and head out."

"Alright. I'll text you if I think of anything."

"Have a good day at work, dear." I smile.

"Bite me."

I smile at my lap while folding my shopping list.

I debate finishing my current chapter like I planned but find my stomach in knots. Some fresh air will help, I'm sure.

Collecting my coat from the dining room chair, I check to make sure I have my keys before exiting into the hall. I miss the elevator at my old apartment, and the telecom to let people in. Granted, I never really used it other than takeout, but the idea of it is still cool. When I first moved in, I remember Amy and I took turns riding the elevator to buzz each other in like we were twelve. Funny how such irrelevant things stay with you the longest.

Crossing the street, I count my blessings that I'm not run over by a car or bicyclist on my way down to the corner store. I take my time walking up and down each isle to avoid bumping into Amy. I recall Logan saying dodging and lying went hand in hand and hate that I feel like he might be right. If I tell Amy and decide not to go, then I'll never hear the end of it, on that same note if I tell her and go then she'll be blowing up my phone the entire time and grill me when I get home. I'd rather decide with a clear head and then fill her in after the fact. It's perfect logic, but I still feel like the world's worst best friend.

Bringing my items to the cashier, I overpay for my generic items and shuffle back out into society. I walk slowly to mull over my new arrangement with Logan. I'm so wishy-washy, one minute I vow to go, the next I'm thinking up sudden illnesses I can pass off as having. When I turn the corner my eyes zero in on the shiny black car that's pulled up in front of the apartment. A uniformed gentleman stands at the passenger door, patiently waiting.

There is no way in hell anyone in this neighborhood can afford wheels like that; given the fact it looks just like the car that picked up Logan Saturday night, I have a distinct feeling this ride is for me. I realize that I haven't made up my mind yet if I'm actually going to go through with this, my thoughts whine on a loop as I cross the street. I avoid looking in the man's direction at all costs, it's highly unlikely that he knows who I am, but I still hurry inside regardless.

THE ART OF DATING

Making it into the apartment, my back pocket buzzes. Setting the bag on the table, I pull out my phone,

LOGAN: I've sent a car to collect you. Should be waiting out front.

ME: I saw. I haven't made up my mind if I'm coming.

I stare at my phone like it's going to bite me when three dots appear.

LOGAN: Wuss. What's the worst that could happen?

ME: I could die.

ME: You might be a cannibal.

ME: I could be chopped into little bits and fed to the birds.

ME: I could die.

LOGAN: The birds can feed themselves, I'm obviously going to sacrifice you to my crate monster under the stairs.

I crack a smile.

ME: I don't know you, you could easily have a crate monster.

LOGAN: His name is Fluffy.

I smile a little harder.

ME: The address you gave me goes to an apartment building.

LOGAN: You're correct. Now, come over; Fluffy's starving.

ME: I don't know.

LOGAN: Wuss.

ME: Shut up. This is self-preservation.

LOGAN: I assume your friend knows of your plans. If you'd be more comfortable, we can move it to a more public setting. I had jumped to the assumption you'd want privacy while discussing our diabolical plan to win Carl back.

ME: His name is Cole.

LOGAN: What would you prefer?

Gah! I don't know.

ME: Hold on.

Opening up a message to Amy I quickly send her a text.

ME: Mr. Money Bags wants to help me win back Cole. He wants me to go to his apartment.

CROTCHSNIFFER: NO WAY!!!!

CROTCHSNIFFER: YOU BETTER NOT BE MESSING WITH ME!!!

CROTCHSNIFFER: DEVINA ANGERSON

CROTCHSNIFFER: *ANDERSON

CROTCHSNIFFER: YOU SAID YES RIGHT.

CROTCHSNIFFER: RIGHT?!?!

I feel like my hand is going to break off from the constant vibration of her mass texts.

ME: I didn't say anything. I don't know him.

CROTCHSNIFFER: Hopefully you'll know him in the biblical sense after this.

CROTCHSNIFFER: OMG MY BEST FRIEND'S GOING TO MARRY A MILLIONAIRE!!!!!!!

ME: Am not. Reread my first text; he wants to help me win back Cole.

CROTCHSNIFFER: WHAT THE FUCK EVER. No, he doesn't. He wants to get into your panties.

ME: Well, that answers that then. Thanks, bestie.

CROTCHSNIFFER: Answers what?

CROTCHSNIFFER: NOOOOOOO.

CROTCHSNIFFER: Don't you dare turn him down!!!!! IM KIDDING!!!! ...well, kinda.

CROTCHSNIFFER: GO!

My phone proceeds to buzz constantly as she sends the word 'GO!' over and over again.

ME: Stooooop already!

CROTCHSNIFFER: What's the worst thing that could happen?

Backing out, I screenshot Logan and I's conversation where he said the same thing and send it to her.

CROTCHSNIFFER: I bet his "Crate Monster" is a euphemism for his dick.

ME: He said its name was fluffy so I really hope you're wrong about that. You're not helping, btw.

64

CROTCHSNIFFER: You're not going to die, Devina. If all you're worried about is your safety, then call me and keep your phone down so if anything bad happens I can call the cops ASAP. If he turns out not to be a murderer you can hang up.

CROTCHSNIFFER: Seriously though. No harm in going over.

ME: Fine.

ME: Be near your phone, his driver's outside and is supposed to take me to his apartment. I'll fwd you the address.

CROTCHSNIFFER: EEEEEEEEEEEEEEP! I can almost smell the money bouquet I'm going to catch at your wedding.

I roll my eyes, returning to Logan's messages.

ME: I'm coming.

LOGAN: I'll see you shortly.

I forward the address to Amy as I descend the stairs. Pushing the door open, the same man stands at the car; I don't think this person has moved at all since I saw him last.

"Excuse me?" He looks up as I approach, "My name's Devina Anderson. Logan said he was sending a car?"

"This would be it. Please," He opens the back door for me, and I have to admit I'm not sure what to do. Do I close it? What if he closes it on me? My thoughts are answered when he politely asks if I'm in. After murmuring a soft 'yes' and 'thank you' he closes it for before moving to take the driver's seat.

The seats are heated leather, and shiny, a very fine layer of grease can be felt as my fingers run over the surface.

"Do you wax your seats?"

"Leather polish, ma'am. It won't stain your clothing."

"Oh, I wasn't worried about that." I chuckle. Pretty sure I've had these jeans since high school. "Just making conversation."

He doesn't reply so I resort to playing with the automatic window. Once I grow bored of that, I shift to the middle seat, leaning into the center console.

"So, like, he's not a murderer or rapist or anything, right?"

He chuckles hoarsely, "No, ma'am."

"Just checking. You'd tell me right?"

"Yes, ma'am."

"What's your name?"

"Caleb, ma'am."

"Cool. I'm Devina."

I see the crows feet deepen with a smile in the rearview window.

"If he murders me, I'm haunting you first," I say, earning me a chuckle. "I'm serious. I'll leave ominous messages on the foggy mirror and hide all your left shoes."

"Mr. Devitt isn't a murderer."

"I'm just giving you the option to save yourself from a haunting."

All I get out of him is another chuckle, so I sit back and watch pedestrians until they begin to fade. The possibility of seeing Cole is slim to none, but I still sink in my seat when we approach my former street. I remain buried in my seat for the duration of Lenox Hill until Caleb turns on 72nd street heading towards 5th Ave.

There's no way; I tell myself sitting upright. Sure enough, we turn on 5th Ave. Shouldering the car in front of a gorgeous brick building, he steps out and opens the door for me.

"You'll need this to access the seventeenth floor." He hands me what looks like a hotel keycard. "Suite A."

"Are you off to get the rubber sheets and hacksaw?"

He smiles, the wear on his face suggests he's in his mid-forties, "Have a pleasant afternoon, Miss Devina. I'll be back to bring you home."

"Home as in my apartment or home like heaven?"

He chuckles, climbing back into the car, leaving me alone.

Sucking in a breath, I tell myself it's courage rather than oxygen and venture inside.

CHAPTER NINE

Holy mother of crap.

Marble floors, crystal chandelier...it's gaudy and uglier than sin; I love it! This is exactly what you see in those cheesy movies; there's even an old woman in pearls with a dog. I refuse to acknowledge the fact it's a service dog because it'll ruin the illusion.

Finding the hideous golden elevator, I rock back on my heels and watch as I get countless side eyes. This is kind of fun. I wonder why Amy and I have never entered into a building just to scope out all the rich people and talk in British accents.

When the elevator opens, I step in followed by three other people, all of them give me an unimpressed once over so you can understand my pure joy when I hold the keycard in front of the little black circle and select the seventeenth floor.

No one glances in my direction again. I feel like a king when the elevator stops on the thirteenth floor, allowing the peasants to get off my damn chariot.

"Cheerio!" I yell through the crack, smiling at myself like an idiot. Quickly pulling out my phone, I take a selfie pointing to the little glowing button of the seventeenth floor and send it to Amy. Within seconds my phone vibrates with her response. I don't have a chance to look at it because the elevator stops, opening to the seventeenth floor. All joy is replaced with trepidation.

Like the good little girl scout, I speed dial Amy and shove the phone into my back pocket. My ratty combat boots sink into the plush maroon and gold carpet as I approach Suite A. Slowly raising my hand, I give it a gentle knock if that's what you could even call it. The roaches in Amy's stairwell knock harder than I just did.

My nerves hit DEFCON 1 when the door opens, revealing Logan in a form-fitting black shirt and designer jeans.

Instead of offering a greeting like a civilized human being, Logan's eyes narrow as he glowers at my outfit, "What the hell are you wearing?"

I glance down at my sweater and jeans, "Clothes."

"If that's what you want to call it." His eyes are glued to my top, "What color is that, mustard?"

"Well, hello to you too."

"That's rough looking."

"Am I expected to stand here and have you mock my clothing or are you going to invite me in?"

"You actually dress like this? Regularly?"

Ugh! What the hell was I thinking coming over here?

"Thanks for the wise words, Logan. I'm sure I'll be able to win Cole back with the supreme knowledge that my clothing sucks." I say, turning around to leave.

His hand snakes around my elbow stopping me, "This is the first time I've seen you outside of a dress, forgive me for being a little shocked." I hear the echo of a familiar laugh leak out of my back pocket.

"Are you done being a jerk?"

He smiles an easy smile releasing my arm before turning to enter his apartment. Half of me wants to get into the elevator and leave, but the other half is incredibly nosy and wants to see what his apartment looks like.

With a loud sigh, I follow him.

"Holy crap." I gasp upon entering.

His place is amazing; floor to ceiling windows, hardwood floors, crown molding, dark, sleek furniture, and a massive kitchen. This is insane.

The view of Manhattan is spectacular. Usually, even in a building this tall, your only view is the building next to you that's just as tall or taller, but not his, he has a clear view over Pilgrim Hill, and it's breathtaking.

A chuckle from the open kitchen draws my gaze; Logan leans against the counter watching me.

"Alright guru, let's get this over with." I groan.

"This isn't a one-day thing; you understand that right?"

"Sure." He has until Thanksgiving after all.

"Have a seat. Can I get you something to drink?"

"Depends. Do you have anything in a can or does Alfred bring you everything in champagne glasses?"

He smiles, "I have both."

"You have an Alfred?!" I crane my neck trying to find a wizened old man in a tux with a towel over his arm.

Logan laughs, bringing heat to my cheeks, "I have cans and flutes, whichever you'd prefer."

"Oh. Well, whatever's easier."

I hear the fridge open as I take in the space. I bet I could fit Amy's apartment six times over in here and still have room to spare. Logan returns with two cans of Coke and a fancy flute glass.

"In the event you wanted both." He smiles, and I feel the tease.

"I think it's a mistake to let me handle anything spillable in here," I say, accepting the can.

He places his drink and the empty glass on a weird circle table between two chairs. It's not big enough to be a coffee table, but not high enough to be an end table. Rich people buy weird things, I decide.

"Please," He waves to the empty chair, "Have a seat."

Pulling my phone out of my pocket, I sit down and stuff the device between my thighs careful not to end the call.

"So tell me about Kurt." He says, sitting down as well.

"His name is Cole, and he's a computer engineer."

"You said you were in a...five?" I nod, knowing where he's going with this. "Five-year relationship."

"Yeah, Amy and I met him at a bar when we first moved here."

"Where'd you move from?"

"Boston."

"What made you want to move?"

"Amy and I made a pact when we were kids to move here, so we did."

"And Amy is the woman from the bar and event at 88 Keys, correct?"

My lap makes a noise as Amy yells into the line. Logan cocks a brow but remains silent.

"Yes. We were neighbors as kids."

He nods before tipping his drink back, "So the computer engineer gets with the book editor."

"Yes," I answer defensively, feeling like his statement is more of a shot at my career than repeating a fact.

"Is he native to the area."

"No, he attended NYU on a scholarship," I announce with pride.

"And the woman he cheated on you with?"

"She was a client of mine."

"An author?" I nod. "Is she well known?"

"Monica Claire, I mean I guess she's well known."

He shakes his head, "Never heard of her." pulling out his phone he begins sliding his finger across the screen while mine continues to murmur between my legs. I'm going to kill her.

"Is this her?" He turns his phone to show a pretty brunette.

"No, may I?" He hands over his phone, backing out I quickly find a photo of the blonde tramp and hand it back. "That's her."

A low whistle escapes his lips as he looks at her perfect image. I used to gush over how pretty she was; full lips with a defined cupid's bow under a straight perky nose and clear blue eyes set off by platinum hair. She's the exact opposite of me where i have mousy brown hair and brown eyes currently hiding behind thick frame glasses without any defining features to set me apart from the next nobody walking down the street.

"She's pretty, I know."

"She's had more work done than Caitlyn Jenner." He says stuffing the phone into his pocket.

My lap once again calls attention as Amy cackles into the receiver. "I'm glad one of you appreciates my humor."

Folding my lips in, I offer an apologetic smile, "I'm sorry. She's here in case of murder."

"In case of murder." He chuckles to himself, before waving to my lap, "Well, cat's out of the bag now. Might as well put her on speaker."

Feeling like a kid caught with their hand in the cookie jar, I remove my phone from my lap and place it on the circular table before pressing the little speaker button.

"Hello, Amy."

"Oh God, I didn't know he could hear me!"

"You were all but shouting," I tell her as Logan smiles.

"I'm sorry!"

"To catch you up, we were discussing Kent and his plastic girlfriend."

"Cole." I correct him yet again.

"That's what I said."

"You called him Kent."

"Oh, well after seeing the Barbie he's playing with, the name Kent seems more appropriate."

"That was Ken." Sometimes I wish I could swallow my mouth to avoid speaking every thought that pops into my mind.

THE ART OF DATING

Logan doesn't seem to mind, he's busy listening to Amy ramble, "Like she even holds a candle to Dee. I mean seriously, the girls about as smart as a box of rocks and as plastic as my nails."

I go to correct that her nails are acrylic but wisely keep my mouth shut. I annoy myself with the need to always correct people so I can assume the feeling is reciprocated tenfold.

"But I mean, look at Dee; she's gorgeous, don't you think?"

My eyes widen in horror as my cheeks heat once again, "Okay!" I say before anyone can say anything else, "Thanks for being my emergency hotline, he's not really putting off any murder vibes, so I'll call you later." Though at the embarrassment she's brought me, I kind of wish he was.

"No, don't hang up!"

"Aren't you at work?"

"Pssht, all these rich Betty's can find their own overpriced handbags, this is much more interesting."

"Goodbye, Ames."

She huffs loudly making Logan chuckle. "Bye, Dee. Bye Mr. Money Bags."

"Bye." He chuckles, I'm glad he seems unaffected by her refusal to use his name.

Ending the call, I offer another apologetic smile, "I'm sorry."

He shrugs, "I cut up my food; you keep your friend on the line while conversing with someone. We all have our quirks."

"I don't usually do that, but I wanted to make sure you weren't serious about your pet monster."

The corner of his mouth raises into another smile, "Don't rule that out just yet, it's still early."

Spinning my coke can in a circle, I gnaw on my bottom lip.

"What kind of things did you and your boyfriend do?"

"I don't know, stuff." I shrug, "We used to go out on the weekends or see a show."

"Just to be clear when you use the term 'we used to' is that past tense because you're separated or because that was at the beginning of the relationship?"

I go to speak when I realize we haven't done any of that in years; we were so caught up with our work that we usually went out separately. "For a moment I thought we were still going out all the time but when you asked that it made me realize that I can't even remember the last time we went out together."

"So what did you do together?"

"Work." I laugh without humor, "We'd order in and watch T.V a lot though."

God, was I really that boring? Maybe I was the one that drove him away after all. Monica was always bragging about her busy nightlife and all the events she was attending.

"What about sex?"

I feel the heat spread up my neck. "What about it?"

He smiles at my embarrassment, "Were you having sex?"

"That's none of your business."

"I'm trying to find the holes in your relationship, so I know where needs work. Sex is pretty important in a relationship."

"There were never any complaints."

"So, no then." He nods, stopping the can I'm still spinning.

"Again, none of your business. Put that in the 'don't need to fix' pile."

"He slept with someone else."

"Really?" I gasp, "I had no idea. All this time I thought they were doing their taxes together."

"Cute." He deadpans.

"It's not up for conversation."

"Fine, we'll come back to that one." I start to protest, but he continues, "I know you're an editor," I nod, "Apart from that, what do you do?"

I offer him a shrug, "Nothing really."

"You can't be that boring, Devina."

"I don't know, depends on my mood."

"So you just sit on the couch all day, every day? You don't have a favorite show or listen to music?"

"Sometimes. I watch what everyone else is watching, and I listen to music if someone puts it on."

"But what do *you* like?"

"I like walking; sometimes I walk around just to watch people in the park. I like to make up stories for them like what they do and where they're going."

"Good, alright what else?"

"What else." I echo, wringing my fingers together.

"It's not hard."

"It is when you have someone telling you you're boring."

"Interests, Devina."

"Sometimes I draw, I don't really watch television because I hate commercials, I prefer movies; nothing specific. Above all, I love to read; books, receipts, magazines, anything with words I'll read."

"Nothing about that's boring. What do you draw?"

"Mostly doodles. When my mind is too occupied or if I'm burned out from editing I'll draw whatever comes to mind to help clear the clutter."

"Are you good?"

"No," A small laugh breaks through the discomfort. "But it helps clear my head."

"The last two times I've seen you, you've been..." His sentence fades as he tries to stifle a smile,

"Well, not like this."

"Amy likes to dress me up like a doll."

"So this," He waves at my body, "Is you normally?"

"Yes." I jut out my chin.

"Are the dorky glasses and weird colored sweaters a statement?"

"No," I glance down, I really don't see anything wrong with what I'm wearing.

"And the," he pauses articulating with his hands around my hair, "Mane and no makeup?"

"I'm clean." I shrug. "Cole always liked the fact I wasn't one of those girls who took nine hours to get ready."

"Are they prescription lenses?" I nod, "This is the first I've seen them, is it safe to assume you have contacts?" I offer another nod, while his eyes look over me in thought.

It feels like I'm standing in front of him naked rather than buried under the safety of my oversized clothing. The way his eyes travel across my body makes me feel insecure like he's making a list of all my flaws.

"Do me a favor, walk to the counter and back."

"Why?"

"I want to see the way you walk."

"What does my walk have to do with getting Cole back?"

"Well if you walk as lazy as you sit, quite a bit."

"I don't sit lazily." I grip, straightening my posture.

He smiles in response before waving towards his kitchen.

Standing up, I twist my sleeve in my hands, "It's going to look weird cause I know you're looking for flaws."

"How do you know I'm not looking for a cheap excuse to check out your ass?"

I crack a small smile at his joke, though self consciously I brush off my pants, and pull my sweater down before walking to the island counter and back.

"Again."

I blow out a breath and do it again.

"Stop being so nervous. I can see it when you walk, just relax. Do it again." I do. "Drop your hands before you twist a hole into that sleeve." Releasing it, I notice the stretched fabric wrinkle and curl at my wrist. "Again."

I walk the distance three more times before he lets me sit down again.

"I think I have everything I need for the time being. Can you come back tomorrow, same time?"

"Um, I'm scheduled for six chapters tomorrow, and I'm already behind on todays. Can I let you know tomorrow?"

"Tomorrow's fine."

"Okay, then. I guess I'll talk to you tomorrow." I say, standing and collecting my still full drink.

"I can take that for you." He offers, but I hold it to my chest.

"That's okay. I'll take it with me."

Walking me to the door, he opens it and leans against the frame, "Until tomorrow."

"Bye."

Walking down the hall, I hear his door close and let go of the breath I didn't know I was holding.

I came in here worried I was going to get murdered and I'm leaving feeling smaller than a grain of dirt. Who would have thought my earlier fear seems like the better option. Selecting the ground floor, I try not to focus on how negative that all felt. If I do, I'm sure to cry, and no one needs that.

Holding my head high, I exit to find Caleb waiting with the back door open, "I'm glad to see you're still alive, Miss Devina."

The noise that comes out of me is part laughing part cry, and I bite my lip to chase the tears as I climb into the back.

He drives me home in silence while I force myself to be a big girl. If Logan can point out that many flaws, how many did Cole notice? Is that why he decided to move her in when I left? Not one call, text, or email with an explanation or apology. My lips trembles as Caleb opens my door; I give him a nod in thanks because if I open my mouth, it's sure to release the dam behind my eyes. Making quick work of the stairs, I lock myself in the apartment. Climbing onto the couch, I hide under a blanket as I did as a child only instead of counting sheep, I'm counting every flaw, bad decision, and every reason I gave Cole to seek out another woman.

The tears flow unchecked while they try to keep pace with the growing number in my head.

CHAPTER TEN

I pulled myself together before Amy got home from work, though puffy eyes and a runny nose are hard to play off with someone who's known you your whole life. She didn't push for information after asking how the day went, no jokes, no pressure, she just climbed onto the couch and gave me cuddles while we binge watched some British show she's into. Before bed she offered me her two-cents, assuring me the first day is always the hardest. The first day of school, of a new job, living alone, it's all the same, but no matter what I decide to do, I'm her favorite person, and she'll support whatever I want to do.

Due to the pity party I threw myself, I didn't finish my chapters for the day, putting me even further behind for the next. This would normally drive me crazy, but I welcomed the inconvenience for the sake of being allowed to cancel Tuesday's classes with Logan without guilt, finishing my book and getting halfway through another wasn't a bad day at all.

Rising with the Wednesday sun, I woke feeling like my skin had grown an extra layer overnight, less bothered by Logan's remarks or my wounded ego. The more I thought about it, the more I realized I'm upset with myself and the person I've become and that my anger was misdirected at Logan. All he did was tease me about my clothing and lack of presentation when it came to my hair and makeup.

Deciding to wear my hair up in a messy bun, I threw in my contacts and dressed in what Amy calls my 'least offense top.' Apparently, it looks super similar to some obnoxiously expensive designer sweater that was all the rave this last fall. I still decide to go without makeup but my skin is clear, and the bags under my eyes are minimal.

"You look well today, Miss Devina," Caleb says, holding the car door open for me.

"Thanks," I smile, getting in.

THE ART OF DATING

I'm sure he meant to say I look like I'm not about to cry like the last time I saw him, but I'm chalking this up to a compliment.

Caleb drops me off once again in front of the white brick building on 5th Ave. I wait by the elevators until one finally returns, scanning the card, I ride up to the seventeenth floor, determined not to let Logan get inside my head. I won't think badly of myself, not again.

Knocking on his door, I wait in the vast hallway until it swings open.

Logan stands in a white button top, black slacks and fancy leather shoes.

Stepping away from the door, he leaves it open as he walks back inside. "I see you've raided Bill Cosby's closet again."

I follow him rolling my eyes at the back of his head. His fingers work down the buttons on his top as he speaks, "I just got in, you'll have to excuse me for a moment. Make yourself at home."

He retreats past the kitchen, entering a hall where the white fabric falls away from his shoulders. My eyes immediately avert to the window. I try not to think about what I just saw, but I mean, I didn't know men had muscles like that on their back. Sure, I read about things like that on fictional characters but never in my wildest dreams did I think I'd see it in real life. I shake my head, hoping to rid the image of his golden skin; those dimples right above his pant line, and the muscle running the length of his spine as if his ass was Moses parting the red sea, but I just can't seem to make it stop playing on a loop.

"Sorry to keep you waiting." I yelp, twisting in his direction. He's changed into a gray shirt, jeans, and basic looking boots.

God, was I really focused on his back that long? Correcting my face, I offer him a polite smile.

"How did editing go?"

"Well," I admit. "Even got a few of tomorrow's finished as well."

"Are you enjoying the author's story?"

"I am, thank you."

Twisting my sleeve, I look back out the window; everything seems so small from up here.

"So from our conversation on Monday, I've compiled a list of things we need to improve."

My stomach drops, I wasn't expecting him to say them out loud. Squaring my shoulders, I face him with confidence only skin deep.

"Have a seat. I forgot to pull it out."

THE ART OF DATING

Forgot to pull what out? He rushes off toward the living room behind me, a moment later, he walks backward pulling a whiteboard on wheels between the kitchen and my seat. Oh, God. He isn't just going to say everything that's wrong with me; he's going to write them down.

Once it's in front of me, he applies pressure to the lock attached to the wheel to keep it in place. It's large enough to cut off my vision to the majority of his kitchen. 'DATING' is printed in large letters across the surface.

"Do I have to call you Mr. Devitt now?" I smile, sitting in the same armchair I used on Monday.

He returns my smile while gathering a marker off the kitchen counter.

"Dating," He starts, "Demeanor," He points to each letter of the word while he speaks, "Appearance, Timing, Infatuation, Negotiation, and my personal favorite, Get Laid." He ends with a wink.

I roll my eyes earning me a glare. "That twitch in your head falls under demeanor, don't be an asshole."

I huff defensively, "My demeanor is fine."

"You're boring." He deadpans me.

"I am *not* boring."

"You have the personality of a wet napkin; you need work."

I keep my head high even though the insult stings, "Cole likes my personality."

"Apparently not. First, we're going to try and find something about you that doesn't suck. Second is appearance," His face curls in disgust as he looks over my outfit, "That's going to be expensive but doable. Third, Timing; after I've fixed your personality and made you relatively pretty we're going to stage a meet with Kode-"

"Cole."

"Whatever, we're going to 'accidentally' bump into him. From this encounter, it's going to launch us right into Infatuation. You're going to be so irresistible at that point he'll be crawling on his hands and knees to get you back, bringing us to Negotiate. That's where you will lay out your list of demands while holding his balls in the palm of your hand. Once he agrees, and he will, you get to Get Laid. Easy."

I have to admit; I'm very fond of I through G. "When do we start?"

"Now."

I take a deep breath knowing he's going to rip me to pieces first and nod. "Then let's begin."

CHAPTER ELEVEN

Logan comes to sit next to me on the opposite chair like last time. "For starters, stop ringing out your sleeves; it showcases your nerves and lack of confidence." My fingers release the strained fabric. "Loosen your arms, open yourself up." Not really sure what he means, I place my hands loosely in my lap. "No, you're doing this," He curls into himself, his shoulders pinch around his neck as he hunches forward, his arms stiff against his lap. "You want to be like this," Pushing his shoulders back, his chest comes forward, his stiff legs loosen to a casual rest as his arms relax. He nods to me, "Try it."

I attempt to recreate his posture to the best of my ability, but it feels forced and uncomfortable.

"Relax, Devina." He smiles, "You're not meeting the Queen. Sit comfortably, but don't fold into yourself. Body language will help with your self-esteem and confidence. Devina, stop fidgeting." My hands still immediately.

"Sorry. It's habit."

"No, you're nervous. Breathe."

I take a deep breath keeping my arms steady.

"Good. Now lift your chin. You already look more confident. Let's work on your posture, raise your shoulders and take a deep breath."

It's weird, but I feel like the air is clearer, my heart seems to be beating at a normal rate and the sweat coating my palm feels thinner.

"With your shoulders back and head held high, you look self-assured and poised; more confident, and in turn, more attractive."

I kind of feel like it too.

"Don't move," He warns when my shoulder begins to drop. "Remember the position you're currently in. This is your homework; I want you to master this, I need it to be your default setting."

THE ART OF DATING

I try to take a mental image of myself. Trying to memorize how I feel in this pose.

"What I've done here is put you in what's called a power pose. Studies have found while practicing a power pose for two minutes you significantly increase your testosterone and lower cortisol levels. When practiced regularly you'll see long-term changes in your confidence. Which is essential in dating; no one wants to be with a pushover with low self-esteem."

I nod, taking another breath. Amy always complains I'm too hard on myself and he's not wrong about the low self-esteem part. Maybe he's onto something here.

Standing up, Logan moves over to the whiteboard, writing 'posture' under the D.

"Does this mean I've aced my first day of training?"

He laughs while shaking his head, "You've been here for less than an hour. Training isn't over yet."

Damn. I was feeling pretty good about myself there for a minute.

He sits back down and looks me over, my heart picking up pace. My shoulders are squared, my chin is up, nothing is crossed or slouching. What am I doing wrong?

The right side of his mouth tips up on the side, "During our conversation, I noticed that not only do you close yourself off to make yourself appear smaller but also that you don't make any direct eye contact. If I move, you'll look at me, but it's always brief. It's important to make eye contact in conversation; you come off truthful and engaging. By always averting your eyes you're not only hurting yourself but the relationships you build." His head tilts to the side while a slow smile grows, "There are those beautiful eyes." I drop my gaze at the compliment, but return to his face when I catch myself, "You need to learn how to accept a compliment." His finger idly taps his bottom lip, "Do you like your sweater?"

I look down at the fuzzy multi-colored stripes, "Yes."

"I don't." I feel my body deflate, why is he always picking on my clothes? "Does the fact we have separate opinions change yours?"

"No."

"The same thing applies when you receive a compliment. You don't have to agree with it for it to be that person's truth. We all perceive beauty differently."

Except he's already more or less told me, I'm ugly. I don't point that out. Instead, I meet his eyes, "Fair enough."

"Straighten your posture."

My shoulders lift immediately, "Sorry."

He waves off my apology as he studies me once again. "Eye contact." He points, "That's where we were. It's important to hold eye contact, stop chewing on your lip when you hold eye contact you're more likely to be assertive and more alluring. If you avert your eyes while someone is speaking, you look bored, and by doing it while you're speaking, you come off dishonest. Eyes, Devina."

I look up, "I don't even realize i'm doing it."

"Hold appropriate eye contact, keep them engaged. You want to mirror their body language, stare and you become creepy." He chuckles when I look away. "Think of it as a speech, you have to take a moment to glance at your cards now and again to make sure you're on track, but you always come back to the audience. Looking away is fine, but make it fleeting. You want the opposite of what you're doing." He laughs.

"Sorry." Slightly adjusting in the chair, I look up at him.

His blue eyes hold mine, "Good. See? It's not that bad, right?"

I smile, glancing at the board, "So, when do we move on to a new letter?"

"This is only the first topic under D. We have a few more. Once you hold yourself the way I want you to, we'll move on."

"Okay." I turn back and make a point to meet his eyes.

I don't know if it's the new power pose or whatever he called it that's making me feel more comfortable in his presence, but I don't feel as shy or awkward when he looks me over.

"Stand up." I obey, "Leave your sleeves alone."

I drop the balled fabric; my hands awkwardly shift between being at my side and crossing at my hips.

Logan starts to laugh, "Just stand still, Devina. You want to come off charismatic. Open yourself, own the air around you, use your hands while you speak. Have you noticed I articulate with my hands? I keep you engaged by making wide motions. When people speak, mirror them; if they're smiling, smile back. If they nod, nod. You become more interesting; you'll draw people in because they view you as personable. Remember your arms and legs while the other person is speaking. By crossing your arms, you suggest your bored or defensive; be relaxed. Your hands are linked, why?"

Unclasping my hands, I shake my head, "I'm not sure."

"You're shy, nervous and maybe uncomfortable, yes?"

"I guess."

"Why?"

"I don't know. This all feels awkward I guess." And it's the truth, all of this feels awkward.

"Do you feel vulnerable?"

"To what?"

"Me, what we're discussing?"

"I don't think so."

"Have you always been socially closed off? You seem to do well when dealing with strangers, yet once you're in a situation where you have to do more than spout witty comebacks you close up. Stop slouching, Devina, stand up straight."

Righting my shoulders I exhale a deep breath, "I guess so. I was a bookworm in school; I didn't participate in group activities unless they were assigned. Amy was always the social butterfly; she has enough charisma and sex appeal to do all the work for me." I crack a smile because it's true.

"Well, that has to change. You need be approachable."

"I don't want to be approachable," I catch myself playing with my sleeve and drop it, "Cole never cared."

"Once he sees the new you, that'll change."

"I don't want a new me," I slouch intentionally, "That's not who he fell in love with."

"Shoulders back. You'll be the same girl; you'll just hold yourself differently. Stop chewing on your lip. When the ugly duckling turned into a swan, it was the same bird right?"

I giggle, "Yes?" I have to admit I've never read the story.

"I'm turning you into a swan, go with it."

A smile fights to break free as I draw my spin straight and raise my chin.

"There you go, ugly duck."

And with that, my smile surrenders. Such an asshole.

CHAPTER TWELVE

Over the last ten days, Logan has shoved posture and conversational skills down my throat to the point it became almost second nature; I find myself sitting straighter, more open rather than curled into a ball over my laptop when editing. During conversations with Amy and Logan, I've caught myself using my hands while I speak and even holding eye contact.

With each small triumph, I find myself more excited for the next day's lesson. Sure, he still drives me crazy and insults me whenever he can, but he's not so bad.

Banging on the bathroom door, I crack it open, "I'm going to Logan's. Want me to pick up something on the way home?"

"I'd kill someone for Chinese!" She calls through the steam.

"Deal, see you tonight."

Collecting my keys and coat from the counter, I skip down the stairwell until I'm approaching the all too familiar black car.

"Hi, Caleb."

"Miss Devina. You seem happy today."

"I'm always happy." I smile, jumping into the backseat. I know I'm a little over the top today, but you would be too if you got signed on for three new manuscripts. Between Logan and Amy feeding me, I'll be able to get an apartment and still have enough left over to furnish it. It's been a good day.

"I used to live down that street," I tell Caleb as we pass through Lenox Hill, I realize I'm no longer ducking in the seat like the weeks before.

"Is that so?"

"Yeah, I got a great deal on rent. Because it's right on the border, I got Midtown price with an Upper East Side address." Doesn't seem like much in NYC but for those in Boston, they view Amy and me as huge successes.

I see the crows feet deepen as he smiles. This is usually how our rides go; I talk, he says something occasionally, and nine out of ten times I'm answered with a polite smile.

"What are you learning today?"

"No idea. Hopefully something new. I'm bored with the whole 'sit straight routine'."

He chuckles while pulling up to the curb. Opening my door, he hands me the elevator keycard. "You'd think I'd have my own card by now." I quip, accepting it.

"Have a good day, Miss Devina."

"You too, Caleb."

"Hi, Harold." I wave at the doorman who looks just as dumbfounded as the first seven times. I'm assuming it's probably because his name isn't actually Harold, that's just what I've decided to call him.

Skipping like a child to the elevator, I press the call button, surprised when it opens almost immediately.

"Whose Grandma had to die to get that one?" Logan eye's my green sweater. I got this one at a second-hand store and I'm confident it's been around since the 80's, so I'm not offended by the jab.

"What are you doing down here?"

"Mail." He dangles a set of keys in front of my face as he passes.

103

"I thought all you rich people got your mail delivered or paid someone to collect it for you."

He chuckles, "I'm capable of retrieving my own bills."

It's weird to think he has those. I mean, of course, he has them, everyone does. But you never hear wealthy people say they have bills to pay or that they'll be late because they have to drop a bill off, ya know?

Skipping behind him, I watch him give me the side eye. I know my demeanor isn't proper but I dare him to say anything about it, I'm going to point out that smile he's trying to hide so fast his head'll spin.

"What's got you in such a good mood, duck."

"I got contracted to three new manuscripts this morning." I smile broadly as he unlocks his box.

"Congratulations."

"Thanks."

Tucking the envelopes under his arm, he locks the little golden door. "How busy will you be with all the new work?"

"It won't be much different than it is now. Maybe an extra hour or two a day." He watches me out of the corner of his eye while we wait for the elevator. "What?"

His lips thin as he shakes his head, "Nothing. Surprised you noticed."

"Why wouldn't I? You're staring at me."

He shrugs, waving me into the empty lift, "Requires eye contact."

"Shut up." I smile, "Whoa, how come you get a cool one?" I motion towards the metal plate attached to his keys that acts like the plastic keycard Caleb gives me.

"Perks of living here."

"I want a cool one."

His face contorts into incredulous humor. "Just an elevator key, Duck. Nothing special."

"Stop calling me that." I give him a mock grump face. The truth is, I'm in an entirely too good of a mood to care about his insulting new nickname for me.

He smiles, watching the little light above the door flash with each floor.

Once the doors open, we walk side by side to his apartment where he lets me in.

"So what's the plan for today?" I ask moving to my chair. When all this is over, I'm probably taking it with me. It already has my butt print permanently embedded in the cushion, fairly certain that's nine-tenths of the law somewhere.

Moving into the kitchen, he produces two Styrofoam containers. YES! Food first. See, today's a great day.

"Today we move on to etiquette."

"To what?"

"Table manners." He answers unimpressed. "Come sit down."

He could tell me to ride the elevator naked, and I'd do it for whatever's creating that aroma. Moving forward quickly, I slide the chair out from the polished oak table and sit down as he delicately transfers the contents onto two plates.

"I know what etiquette is, but why are we doing it?"

He stops mid-movement, "You're kidding right?"

"No, why? What's wrong with the way I eat?"

"Everything."

"Not true." I protest.

"Devina, you morph into this ravenous creature whenever you're around food. I'm surprised you even taste what you're eating with how quickly you consume it."

"It's meant to be eaten."

"Yes, eaten. Not crammed down your throat in record speed. I know many things; the Heimlich maneuver isn't one of them."

"Okay, so what? Just eat slower?"

"That and breathing between bites for starters."

He sets a plate down in front of me, and my mouth begins to water. A thick steak with weird colored toppings, mashed potatoes, and these long tiny carrots stare back at me. I'm going to make this plate my bitch.

He also sets a fancy folded napkin, silverware and a champagne glass in front of me. Once he's pleased with the appearance of everything, he takes the seat across from me.

"Depending on where you're eating the rules change. Seeing as this is indoor, we'll treat it as a private dinner party."

"How fancy."

"First, remove your forearms from the table." He smiles as I comply without argument, "Food motivated are we?"

"You have no idea."

He chuckles softly. "Okay, so when you are seated you sit politely until the host removes their napkin, at which time you will mirror that person." Reaching forward, he selects the folded maroon cloth and lays it across his lap. I snicker, I didn't know men did this, I thought that was only a lady thing. Still, I mirror him. "Same logic when it comes to dining, once the host picks up their cutlery you may as well. You work from the outside in, so the fork furthest from your plate is what you use first." He picks up his fork and knife, I mirror him, "At a slow and relaxed speed, cut a few, small, bites before setting your knife down," I again follow his lead. I'm about to take this plate to the elevator if he doesn't hurry this little tutorial up. He sets his knife down, fighting a smirk.

"Is this small enough?" I ask, looking down at my plate

"That's fine. The point of smaller pieces is not only to be polite and look like a civilized human being, but in the event someone speaks to you, you won't struggle to swallow before answering."

I snort, "I just talk around it."

"I know." He deadpans, making me laugh.

"Bring your food to your face, don't hover over your plate like an animal. Chew slowly and quietly."

"I don't smack my food." I gripe, spearing a square of perfectly pink meat.

"No, but your jaw pops. Most likely because you're dislocating it in the process of cramming everything in at once."

I smile into my fork, before taking a bite. Mother of crap this is delicious.

"Good?"

"Very."

"See? You were able to answer without spitting food everywhere."

"Shut up. If my mouth is full, I put my hand up to avoid that. I'm not an animal."

"Are you sure about that? I'm certain I've seen starving dogs eat slower than you." I roll my eyes, earning myself a glare. "They're going to roll right out of your head if you keep that up."

I smile a cheeky grin, before taking another delicate bite.

Following his lead, I clean my plate without criticism. Just to torment him I place my silverware across my plate and at an angle, signaling I'm finished.

His brow raises, "Well, would you look at that. I didn't think it was possible, to be honest."

"What? That I know a thing or two about table manners?"

"No, that you were capable of eating like a lady."

"Shut up. I have manners when it counts, not that I'll ever be in a position to use them. The fanciest meal I'll be having is at a steakhouse where my fork and knife are wrapped in a paper napkin." I laugh, "But it was fun pretending. I was half tempted to mess up so that you'd force me to do this every day rather than practice sitting or speaking."

He chuckles, standing to collect our plates.

"So, now that that's done. What's next?"

Pulling myself to my feet, I follow him into the kitchen.

"To be honest, I expected this to take much longer."

"It's my goal in life to surprise you," I say, twirling in a circle like an ungraceful ballerina.

"Feeling confident are we?"

I laugh, using the counter to steady my dizzy head. I offer a weak shrug, "Eating, it's kind of my forte."

He laughs, drying his hands on a nearby towel. "Alright, Miss Confidence. Let's put your training to the test."

"Written or verbal?" I tease with a grin.

"Tomorrow night I take you out. If you pass, we'll move on. Fail, and we continue conversational skills."

I feel my face curl; I hate conversational skills. "Promise?"

He nods once, "You have my word."

I smile triumphantly, "Letter 'A' here we come."

CHAPTER THIRTEEN

The moment Amy learned about mine and Logan's dinner test, she jumped at the opportunity to dress me. I received a text an hour ago informing me I was to wear a dress. Any ugly sweaters would be an automatic failure.

Wearing a pair of low heel black pumps, Amy loaned me a simple maroon dress, probably the classiest thing she owns.

Angling my head lower, I hear the hiss of her flat iron as it straightens my waves into satin sheets.

"Do you know where you're going?"

"Nope, just that I had to wear a dress."

"It's kinda hot, ya know. This whole Cinderella story."

My brow furrows, "How is this a Cinderella story? He's helping me get Cole back."

I can practically hear her eyes rolling, "Cole doesn't deserve you. I'm totally shipping you and Logan."

I bark out an incredulous laugh, "Prepare yourself for disappointment then. Logan's alright I guess, but I doubt we'll stay friends when this is all over. The guy hates everything about me."

"He does not."

"He asked if I was homeless the other day." I deadpan.

She speaks with an angelic laugh, "I'm with Logan on that one, I've been saying you dress like a bum for years."

"There's nothing wrong with my clothes."

"Except the fact you're hidden under them."

"It's cute."

"Some are." She agrees, "Like that navy sweater that hangs off your shoulder, if you paired it with something other than ripped leggings it could be super cute. Too bad your ass can't squeeze into my jeans."

I chuckle, working the stick of mascara through my lashes once again. Ames already did my makeup, but I need something to occupy my nervous hands. "They don't stand a chance."

"I know, if they did, I would have thrown your gross leggings away the second you moved in." She smiles, unplugging the flat iron. "Alright, let me look at you."

Standing, I let her look me over, spinning when she signals me with the twirl of her finger. "Perfect."

"Were you able to find that jacket?"

"Oh, crap. I forgot to look. Hold on; I'll be right back."

Ducking past me she heads to her room while I collect my phone off the charger in the living room.

LOGAN: T-minus thirty minutes.

"He said he'd be here in thirty minutes, thirty minutes ago," I yell, typing out a message to him,

ME: A skirt works right?

LOGAN: Sure.

ME: Cool. Ames tried getting me into a dress, but I had this adorable top I wanted to wear instead.

LOGAN: If it's an ugly sweater be prepared for fourteen days of talking. I'll get creative; speech, pronunciation, mouth movement.

ME: What if it's a sweater, but it's really cute paired with a skirt?

LOGAN: I think we'll start with the letter A, and work our way through the dictionary.

I smile at the screen when a knock sounds at the door.

"I'll get it!" Amy shouts from the depths of her closet, even though I'm literally three feet from the door.

ME: How about I wear the sweater and if you don't like it, I'll change?

Amy comes barreling out of her bedroom with a black fabric coat draped over her arm, "Quick, how do I look?" She stage whispers in front of the door.

"Hot as always." Her lips curl into a seductive smile, "I don't know what you're worried about, it's just Caleb."

"Never know."

I don't have time to respond before she yanks the door open, "Mr. Devitt."

"What?" I slip behind her frame to gaze over her shoulder, "Logan actually came up?"

"If you're in a sweater I might be forced to burn everything you own."

Amy pushes the door wider, allowing Logan to step in. He looks every bit the millionaire in his dress slacks, white shirt, and blazer thing; he looks ridiculously hot. I'm his friend; I'm allowed to think that.

"Your mission in life to surprise me is on the fast track, Miss Anderson. I wholeheartedly believed you, oh, woman of no lies." He gives me a pointed look.

"I didn't lie. I wanted to wear a skirt and Amy tried to get me in a dress. I never specified who won the argument. I also used the term, 'what if.'" I smile.

"You look lovely; I'm glad the dress won. Am I to thank you for the total package?" He turns to Amy who actually blushes.

"She picked the shoes."

He glances at my feet before thanking her for her 'hard work.' I roll my eyes in an exaggerated fashion, disappointed when it goes unseen.

"After you." He waves to the door.

Amy reaches forward with my coat, but Logan takes it from her, holding it out for me to slip my arms into.

"How chivalrous."

"God, could you guys be any cuter?" Amy swoons.

116

"Oh, slow your libido, it's not a date."

"Sure, sure." She waves me away, "Have her home by midnight and not a minute later."

"Yes, ma'am. I promise to be on my best behavior."

"I wish you wouldn't."

My incredulous "Ha!" echoes down the stairwell as I step outside.

Logan and I descend in comfortable silence.

"Stop it," I tell him, when he holds the main door open for me, "You'll give a girl expectation doing things like that." He rolls his eyes as I pass, "They're going to roll right out of your head if you keep doing that."

He chuckles, stepping up to my side to open the car door, "You're a bad influence on me."

"Pssht! I'm great if anything I'm improving you."

Stepping into the car, I scoot over to the far window, giving Logan room to slide in beside me.

"I could have walked around."

"Now you don't have to. Hi, Caleb. How was your day?"

"Miss Devina," He nods in the mirror, "It was exceptional, how was yours?"

I giggle at his reply, "It was fine. What about you Logan? How was your day?"

117

"Busy." He smiles, "Meet your chapter quota?"

"No, but I can make them up tomorrow. Where are we going?"

"A restaurant."

"Shocking."

Logan smirks, giving me a sideways glance.

"Hey, Caleb, where are we going?"

His response is to tap his nose.

"Traitor." I groan, sitting back in the seat.

I have to fight the urge to slouch; no way am I messing up tonight. I even googled fancy restaurant etiquette to ensure I pass Logan's test. If I never hear the term, 'shoulders back,' again, it'll be too soon.

"You're fidgeting," Logan notes.

"Am not, how?"

He nods to my tapping finger on the armrest.

"I'm tapping to the beat of the music, listen."

My finger continues to beat to the soft hum of music pouring from the front seat.

"I stand corrected."

Silencing my finger, I wait out the drive in silence.

We pull up outside what looks like a posh hotel. "Here?"

THE ART OF DATING

Logan nods as Caleb exits his place to open my door.

I wait patiently, standing to my full height as Logan exits the car, buttoning his jacket; he looks like he's in a cologne commercial.

"Is this where you offer me your arm?" I tease, falling into step with him, he smirks, his hand falling to my lower back to guide me inside. I tense at the contact; Logan and I don't touch.

He escorts me to an elevator where an attendant waits.

I try to hide my giddiness when the old man enters behind us and selects a floor marked, R. It takes every ounce of self-control not to speak to him. I'm beyond curious about this man dressed in black dress pants and a red jacket similar in style to Logan's. I also want to ask if they're hiring because this seems like job goals.

All too quickly the doors open, the sounds of clinking china finds my ears right as the vast floor is uncovered by the opening doors. Dim bulbs light the restaurant, drawing the New York skyline into focus outside the floor to the ceiling windows.

Logan murmurs something to the balding butler-host guy behind the podium while I remind myself to stand up straight which is proving to be difficult when a woman dripping in flashy jewelry walks past me; I feel underdressed and out of place.

Logan's hand gently pushes against my lower back, ushering me to follow the balding man. I'm all too aware of his fingers our entire journey to a table against the window.

Calling all of my googled knowledge forward, I wait for Logan to pull out my chair. He takes it one step further when his fingers clasp the collar of my jacket, slowly peeling it away. The butler guy takes it from him, freeing his hands to pull out my seat, "Thank you."

He smirks, moving to his seat.

My confidence starts to waver when I note we have three empty glasses instead of two, every diagram I looked at, specifically had two; water and a wine glass.

Logan lays his napkin across his lap, and I follow suit, "Logan." I say gently, trying to keep my volume low like the other patrons. His eyes lift to mine, "Why are there three glasses? I thought there was only supposed to be two."

He smiles a genuine smile, "Two of them are wine glasses. Depending on what wine is served, they'll remove one of them."

"Oh." I gently rest my hands in my lap, "Did I get docked points because of that?"

His smile widens, "No."

The waiter comes over, handing Logan a leather book.

He proceeds to say something I can't pronounce and sends the man away.

"This view is incredible," I note, attempting to strike up polite conversation.

"I agree."

"Have you been here before?"

The corner of his mouth raises slightly, "Once or twice."

The waiter returns pouring a soft yellow liquid into his glass. After Logan takes a sip, he nods to the waiter who fills both of our drinks, leaving the uncorked bottle in a flashy chrome container next to the table. Producing two pieces of rectangular cardstock, he hands them to Logan and I. This is probably the smallest, yet most complicated menu I've ever seen.

"Is this English?" I ask in all honesty.

Logan chuckles. The title of each plate isn't in English, but the short description below it claims to be. I catch keywords like duck and venison, but everything else is out of a Dr. Seuss classic.

"Would it be rude to ask you to order for me?"

121

He smiles again, "If you want, I could also tell you what each dish is as well."

"I trust you."

I'm thankful when he reaches for my menu; I didn't read anything about where to put it. The waiter returns allowing Logan to order in what sounds like French.

"Do you speak French?" I ask when the waiter retreats.

"I do. My mother insisted on a second language when my sister and I were young."

"That's neat, my dad's French."

"Is that right? Did he teach you?"

"No, I've never met him, I'm the product of a summer romance." I smile, "She married someone when I was young, and he took over the role though."

"Do you get along with your parents?"

I nod, making sure to look into my glass when I sip my wine. "They live in Boston. Amy and I go back once a year to see our families."

"Any siblings?"

"Nope. I'm an only child, though with Amy and I being friends since we were in kindergarten, my parents look at her as a second child. You mentioned a sister earlier, is she older or younger?"

"Older. She's an event coordinator here in New York."

"Well, that sounds like a fun job."

"She enjoys it."

I'm surprised when the waiter returns, placing our entrees in their designated spot. Logan cut's into the thick chunk of meat in the center of his plate, "Wonderful, thank you."

"That was fast," I comment, following Logan's movements.

"Perks of being rich." He smiles.

Rolling my eyes, I dig in.

At the end of the night, I can't wipe the smile off my face as we head back to my apartment. Not only did I pass his test with flying colors, I actually had a wonderful time. After our meal, we were served this crazy desert hidden under a chocolate shell, the waiter poured this hot red goo over it, and it broke away to reveal a cheesecake. It was odd but delicious; if I weren't fighting to pass his test, I would have licked the plate clean.

"Did you enjoy your evening?" Logan asks on the ride home.

"I did." The absence of light makes his eyes appear almost black, every so often we pass by a light that gives me just a glimpse of color. "Thank you for choosing to test me."

"It was my pleasure." He smiles.

All too soon the car pulls up outside Amy's apartment. Logan exits first, holding the car door open as I slide out, careful not to let my dress ride up.

"Until tomorrow?" I ask when he doesn't move from the sidewalk.

His head angles toward the entrance, and I follow, "A gentleman sees her to her door."

"You don't have to do that." I chuckle. "Here's fine. Tomorrow?"

He nods once, allowing me to enter the building, "Have a good night, Devina."

"Night." I smile shyly, turning for the stairs.

As I make my way up to Amy's, I laugh at myself. This was hands down, the best not date, date I've ever had.

CHAPTER FOURTEEN

Unfortunately, Logan was called away for an impromptu business trip to China. So I've spent the last two weeks cooped up inside working on manuscripts. Business is booming for me at the moment, so I'm not complaining. If you had told me two months ago that I would have a steady income I would have laughed, yet here I am, raking in the money. Well, maybe not raking but a win's a win.

Needing a change of scenery, I wandered down to a coffee shop to work on the last chapter of the current manuscript I'm editing.

Grabbing my buzzing phone off the counter, I smile at the notification bar. Unlocking my phone, I open my messages.

LOGAN: [Attachment]

A second text vibrates in my hand while the image downloads.

LOGAN: Look, Bev Goldberg's in a coffee shop.

The photo blinks to life, showing me sitting cross-legged in the booth, with the oversized cup tipped against my lips.

My head swivels to the window, searching for a certain stalker.

"Hey, Duck." I yelp, spinning in his direction causing him to laugh. "Miss me?"

"Hey!" I smile, watching him sit in the seat across from me. "What are you doing here?"

"I went to your apartment, but you weren't home. Amy sent me here."

"I needed to get out of the house," I admit, closing my laptop to see him better. "How was your trip?"

"Long." He chuckles, "Overall, successful though."

"Well, that's good. Do you want me to flag down the waiter?"

He shakes his head, "No, that's alright. What are your plans for the day?"

"I don't have any."

He offers a curt nod, "Good. Class is back in session. Once you're finished, we'll run your items home."

I smile, slamming the contents of my coffee down, "Done."

Throwing a few bills on the table, I collect my jacket as Logan takes the laptop from me.

"What's the plan?"

"You've been promoted to the letter A; appearance. Want to guess where we're starting?"

"My sweaters," I grumble, standing up.

"Yes, ma'am." He inhales like he's about to speak again but stops short.

Looking up at him, I wait for him to continue but he doesn't, he just stares.

"What?" I ask, wiping my mouth on my sleeve, "Do I have something on my face?"

"No, you look fine." Whatever caused his momentary stall obviously passes when a mask clouds his features, "Let's go, Duck."

I hate that nickname. He holds the door for me as we step outside.

"I don't have to like throw my stuff away or anything, do I?"

He pulls back slightly, "Of course not. But with any luck, you'll do that on your own admission."

"Doubtful."

He chuckles, stopping at the curb.

"I'm this way." I point out when he doesn't walk with me.

With a simple nod of his head, I see Caleb a few cars back.

"You know we could walk right?"

"Not where we're going."

"I thought we were taking my stuff back?"

"I'll have Caleb take it to your apartment."

"Are you driving me home when we're done?" He gives me an exasperated nod, "Then we can leave it in the car. Amy has to work today, so nobody's gonna be home anyway."

Once the car gets close enough, Logan ushers me into the street, where we both jump in quickly to avoid being run over by impatient drivers.

"Hi, Caleb."

He nods in the mirror, too occupied with his attempts not to run anyone over.

"So, is this going to be like an episode of What Not to Wear?" I ask Logan.

"Pretty much."

"Cool. I haven't been shopping in forever."

"Since the eighties at least."

"I wasn't even born in the eighties."

"I know, Duck."

Jeez. I've been in his presence for all of fifteen minutes, and he's already annoyed with me.

"Why do you keep calling me that?" He starts to smile and I know he's about to insult me, "Never mind, I already know; ugly duckling. How do you manage to keep friends when you're always insulting them?"

"I don't insult my friends; I insult you."

I scoff, "You're such an asshole."

"You mispronounced honest."

"I haven't seen you in two weeks the least you could do is be nice to me."

"I'm always nice to you; you just don't see it."

"When?" I demand.

"Well, I think this boot camp to win Joel back is pretty generous."

"Cole and I'm not some charity case. You offered, remember?"

"You're my pro bono case." He nudges my shoulder with his, wearing a teasing smile.

Rolling my eyes, I nudge him back.

"So where are we going?" I've got some spending money burning a hole in my pocket making me excited for this impromptu shopping trip.

"A few places. The first is right up here."

129

THE ART OF DATING

Inside I deflate a little; this is Upper Manhattan aka the expensive, designer brand area.

"I was hoping for an Old Navy or Macy's."

He laughs hard and loud enough to grind on my nerves. "Not a chance. You think I'd take you to sweater heaven?"

"They sell other things." I pout, looking out the window.

We stop in front of one of those boutiques with a revolving door looking every bit like 1960's New York.

"Come on, Duck, let's try and make you pretty."

I think I might hate him.

CHAPTER FIFTEEN

By 'a few places' he meant seven. I've been carted around for the last three hours, dressed and undressed by prissy old ladies just to have Logan veto everything I'd been stuffed into. Not that I'm complaining, at one point I was wearing a jacket covered in peacock feathers, but something's got to give eventually.

This new attendant has her hands full; running around like a chicken with head cut off, trying to shop for three different customers. I'm not bothered by her delay; I get to sit in a comfortable chaise lounge, sipping champagne like a rich person rather than be told I don't look good in anything I try on.

"If you wanted results, you should have just taken me to Perkins and had Amy dress me."

"You'd con your way into getting your way, and we both know it." He smiles, shaking his head. "Isn't this what girls like? Being waited on and dressed head to toe?"

"Amy? Absolutely. Me? Not so much. I'd rather rummage through the clearance rack and be done with it."

"You don't say."

"Shut up. Oh look she's back. Should we just go ahead and send her away because you're going to say no to everything I put on anyway?"

I'm given a scolding look as she approaches, red-faced and out of breath, "I'm so sorry. Right, this way."

Handing my glass to Logan, I follow her until we're behind the privacy curtain. Moving against the wall, I give her room to straighten the trolley full of colorful clothing. "Mr. Devitt said you were looking for casual, business casual, dinner party and event."

"I don't know about all that other stuff, but casual works for me."

"I was instructed pullover sweaters were completely off the table, but I did find a few cardigans I think you'll like."

Pulling a string of hangers from the pole, she instructs me to change. Patiently handing me each item as I go; it's a good thing I'm not a shy girl.

Slipping my feet into a pair of ballet flats, I'm once again carted out to Logan.

Knowing the drill, I pause before turning around.

"Jeans and shoes can stay. That top makes you look flat chested."

"I am flat chested."

Ignoring me, he points down the hall, "Change."

Like the little doll I am, I obey, but not before giving him an exaggerated eye roll.

Halfway through the trolley and we still haven't made any progress.

"Oh, these aren't the right shoes." She says, staring at the pair of maroon pumps. "I'll be right back, go ahead and get in the dress while I'm gone."

I don't even have a chance to nod before she slips out of the room.

Pulling the yellow dress from the hanger, I step into it, hauling the material up my torso and tucking my arms into the sleeves. It's very pretty; lace top to bottom. The only negative is I can't wear a bra with it due to the fact the sleeve rides the very edge of my shoulders.

Reaching blindly behind me, I follow the seam of the zipper just to come up empty-handed. Not even my reflection offers assistance.

Popping my head out of the curtain, I search for the attendant.

"What do you need?" Logan asks when he notices me.

"Nothing," I sigh, not spotting the girl anywhere, "You're just going to say no anyway so I doubt it matters." Stepping out, I hold the back together with my fingers.

"Put your arms down."

"I can't; I'm holding the back shut." His puzzled features prod me to continue, "I think the zipper's broken or something, I can't seem to find it."

"Here, turn around." He says standing.

Once my back is to him, I let go of the fabric.

My nerves start to rise when his fingers brush against the bare skin of my back. I'm all of a sudden very aware of how exposed I am; not only am I braless, but the zipper sits right above my buttcrack, and I'm not exactly wearing modest underwear.

I'm acutely aware of every movement he makes in his attempt to locate the zipper, once he finds it, the material molds against my frame the higher it climbs, his fingers drawing a burning line up my spine.

I feel his hands leave my body before I look up, catching his reflection in the mirror across the hall.

"There you are." He appears almost impressed.

"Thank you." Ew, why I do I sound like that? All whispery and dry.

Clearing my throat, I turn around to face him.

His earlier expression replaced with bored features that match his dull tone, "Shoes?"

"She grabbed the wrong pair; she'll be back."

His eyes roam the fabric while he chews on the inside of his lip.

"Might save time if I just took it off and moved on to the next thing," I tell him, annoyance leaking from each word.

"I didn't say anything."

"No, but you're going to. Just like you've been doing all day. You drilled it into my head that I needed to stand a certain way to feel confident, yet here you are telling me I look like crap in everything I try on."

135

"I haven't used that term once and at no point have you disagreed with me."

"What's the point of disagreeing with you?"

"I'd assume you'd want a say in what you wear. You're a very vocal person, Devina." He says, sitting back down.

"I want to wear oversized sweaters and leggings."

"No."

"See?"

"Tell me your thoughts on this," He points to my dress.

"I think it's pretty."

"Would you wear it?"

I shrug, "Yeah, I mean I don't wear dresses often, but when Amy drags me out, I'd wear it."

"And if I don't like it?"

"Then it goes into the never-ending no pile."

His brow furrows, "Have you been silent this entire time because you believed what I said was final?"

"Well, yeah." I throw my hands.

"Devina." He deadpans, disbelief clouding his features. "I'm giving my opinion not telling you what you can and can't have. Well, apart from estate sale sweaters."

Irritation grows in my stomach, webbing its way up my throat, "Are you saying we could have been done hours ago?"

"If you were fond of something, yes."

Dropping my hands against my waist, I glare at him. "You didn't think to tell me I was allowed to choose?"

"I didn't know I needed to. You're a grown woman; this is an exercise to show you what's flattering to your figure so when you're rummaging through the clearance racks, your words, not mine, you'll be able to dress without looking like a beggar."

Closing my eyes, I count back from ten, "In that case, when she gets back, we're leaving."

"Have you completed her catalog?"

"I don't speak rich, dumb it down."

The right side of his lip raises, "Have you tried on everything she brought in with you."

"Oh, no. But it's just dresses left."

He nods, turning to look at the approaching attendant.

"Again, I'm so sorry, here are the shoes," She hands me a pair of purple pumps, that I quickly slip into.

I never thought yellow and purple would match, but it looks surprisingly good. "I like it."

"Good." Logan pipes up behind me, "Let the attendant know what you're keeping."

"Will do," I call over my shoulder, walking back into the changing room, more than ready to call it a day. The longest day of my life and I could have been done at the first store.

Rolling my eyes at myself, I quickly change and start separating the clothing I like onto the empty rack behind me when the attendant returns.

"Can you arrange these by price?"

"Excuse me?"

"You know like cheapest to most expensive? I couldn't find any price tags."

She stammers a moment, looking between me and the clothing. "I don't understand. Mr. Devitt said price wasn't an issue."

"Yeah, well, Mr. Devitt isn't the one with a budget here."

Her mouth continues to open and close like a fish; I don't get the confusion.

"You're paying?"

"Well, yeah." I chuckle. "Who else woul-" My question dies as the pieces start to fall into place, "No," I draw slowly, he wouldn't. "What did he tell you when I was changing?"

"To charge the clothing to his account," She says slowly.

138

"Okay. Well, let's not do that. Just arrange these for me, and I'll be right back."

Swiping the curtain away, I stomp down the hall towards him, "You're not buying me clothes."

His eyes widen in surprise at my attitude, "Why not?"

"Because I can buy my own damn clothes. I know we joked about me being a charity case in the car, but it was just that; a joke. I don't need your damn charity."

"You didn't have a problem with this before."

"I wasn't aware this was the plan." I cross my arms over my chest.

"In the beginning, I said it would be expensive but doable." He says standing. My sudden anger keeps me planted to the spot even though we're now nose to nose. "Plus, I can afford it."

"And I can't?" I spit in offense.

"Can you?"

Scoffing, I swallow the urge to hit him, "You're a bastard. I may not live in some fancy apartment and have more money than sense, but I can affor-"

"Do you want Carl back?" He interrupts.

"His name is Cole; how many times do I have to-"

"Yes or no?"

"Yes, but that gives you no right to-"

"Then play by my rules."

"Stop interrupting me!"

He shrugs. "Stop throwing a tantrum."

"I am not throwing a tantrum. Calling me ugly and mocking my fashion sense is one thing, but treating me like I'm worthless is on another level."

"When have I ever treated you like you were worthless?" He challenges, encroaching on my personal space further.

"Right now! You doubted the fact I could afford an outfit just because we're in some rich-bitch store."

"That dress you were wearing costs three grand." He keeps his tone even while I feel all the blood leave my body, "Now understand why I would ask if you can afford it. Three grand is nothing to me, where that's at least two months' rent for you."

Swallowing, I try to think of a way out of this with my pride intact. Three grand for a piece of fabric?

"You agreed to do this my way." His eyes follow my jaw before boring into mine once again, "My way includes buying you shit, get over it."

"And what does this get you? Spending money on a person and getting nothing in return?" I ask trying to hold onto my anger; if I let it go, I'm going to feel like a chastised child.

"We have a bet going; this gets me the win."

"Cole's never cared about what I wore or what I looked like."

"That's because he was too busy caring what other women looked like naked."

Heat surges under my skin, "That's *not* true."

"You know," He cocks his head to the side, the tip of his nose brushing against mine, "You're kind of hot when you're angry."

"You're a pig."

His lip starts to raise, "And you're not pulling away."

"I hate you." Taking a step back, air chills my face. It hadn't dawned on me just how close we were until he pointed it out.

"We'll take it all." He says, looking over my shoulder.

Embarrassment creeps up my neck as my eyes land on the attendant standing not three feet away from us; witness to our little tiff.

"Logan," I growl.

Leaning into my space, I retreat earning me a smile, "My class, my rules."

He pulls away, not bothering to look back as he retreats.

Turning slowly, I approach the woman. Grabbing the yellow dress, I pull it off the trolley. "Maybe we don't get this one."

CHAPTER SIXTEEN

How would I describe my week? Well, annoyed sums it up pretty well.

After Logan and I had our little outburst, I've refused to go back over. A carrier delivered my clothing, yellow dress included, a few hours after I got home. If it weren't for Amy's love of fashion, they would have gone completely untouched. My attempts to return them were denied by the establishment leaving me feeling guilty. He wasted so much money on things I don't need, and my pride is a glaring brick wall standing in the way of accepting them. I haven't even thanked him yet, how ungrateful is that?

"You going to Logan's?" Amy asks walking out of the bathroom, her finger fumbling to secure her earring.

"Nope."

"Come on, Devina." She sighs, "So the guy acted like an asshole? What's new?"

"He's normally teasing, Ames. He made me feel like Cole's mistake was my fault because I'm ugly. He hurt my feelings." And he did. Apart from my embarrassment and wounded pride, his accusations about Cole hurts the most.

"Stop calling it a mistake. That sorry s-o-b is living with her, in your apartment. He didn't do it because you're ugly, which you're not, he did it because he's a piece of shit."

"We agree to disagree, and we don't know that they're still together."

"They were the last time I was on Facebook."

My face curls as that hole in my chest aches, "You're stalking him?"

"No, he blocked me. I am stalking her though. They bought new dishes the other day."

Thumping my head against the back of the couch, my mood depletes further; spilling out of my body and staining the cushions with my misery. "I don't want to know that."

"You need to accept it." She says zipping her jacket.

144

"You look nice by the way," I tell her, appreciating the Jennifer Aniston thing she's got going on.

"I know. You need to call Logan."

"Have a good day."

"I'm serious, Dee."

"We need shampoo."

Growling, she shakes her head, "I'll see you tonight."

Pulling the door open, she yelps.

"Is Devina here?"

"Logan?" I pull myself off the couch to look over Amy's shoulder. Sure enough, Logan stands outside the door. "What do you want?"

"You've had a week to lick your wounds; we have work to do."

"Yeah, I'm not going."

Amy squeezes past him, murmuring "Apologize" before entering the stairwell.

"You're still upset?" His brow furrows in concern.

"Of course I'm still upset."

"Because I bought you clothing?"

"The clothes are just hurt pride, the comment about Cole is what I'm upset about."

"And what comment would that be?"

"You said Cole cheated on me because I'm ugly."

145

"I said no such thing." He tells me, entering the apartment, uninvited.

"Yes, you did. You said he didn't care what I looked like because he was checking her out or whatever."

"Mhm, and where in that statement did I call you ugly?"

"You implied it."

"I did not." His calm demeanor is frustrating.

"Yes, you did."

"Devina, I wouldn't imply it because I don't believe it. He cheated because he couldn't see what was in front of him, I'm making him notice."

"Well, your efforts are pointless now. They're living together."

His brow lifts, "How do you know that?"

"Amy stalks the girl's Facebook."

A smile tugs at his lips, "But not you?"

"No, not me. That's not something I want to see."

"You've mentioned that your friend disapproves of you returning to the relationship," I nod, though the word 'disapproves' is a tad mild, "How do you know if what she says is true?"

"Because she wouldn't lie about it." He quirks a suspicious brow, "She wouldn't."

"Let's test this theory," He waves towards the couch.

"You want to test to see if Amy's lying?"

"Lying is too harsh of a word; I want to see the difference in perception."

"Dumb it down."

"Just bring up the girl's Facebook."

"Logan," I sigh, "I don't want to see it."

"You don't have to." He pulls out his phone, taking a seat on the couch, "What's her name?"

"Monica Claire." Moving over to the couch, I sit beside him.

"Which one?"

Angling the phone in my direction, my heart aches at her new profile picture. "That one."

I point to the image of her and Cole, snuggled close together.

"Okay," He says, idly scrolling. "Wait, that's not him?"

Glancing at his screen, I nod, confirming the photo he's on is Cole.

"Him? The guy who looks like his parents are related?"

I crack an unwanted smile, "He does not. He's attractive."

"For a product of incest, sure."

147

"Don't be mean."

"You're a bit out of his league, don't you think?" He says, squinting at the photo.

"You've got that backward, just look who's he with; she's gorgeous."

"That's a matter of opinion."

I don't bother replying as he gets lost in her profile.

"You look miserable in your profile picture." He says after a while.

I stop picking at my nails, looking at him, "Are you on my Facebook?" He nods, "Why?"

"Call it curiosity. Sent you a friend request, approve it. Only cool kids get to be friends with me."

"How did you even find me?" I ask, opening my laptop.

"You commented on one of her photos."

Logging into my account, I'm shocked at the number of notifications. "Someone's popular." He says, looking over my shoulder.

"I haven't been on since I walked in on them."

"Change your profile picture while you're on there."

"Why?"

"Because it's sad. Put this one up." He shows me his screen, revealing a photo of Amy and I dancing on a bar from my cousin's bachelorette photo last summer.

"That's old, plus it's not exactly the message I want to be sending when potential clients look me up."

He shrugs, his fingers continuing to swipe at the device.

When Cole changed his status to single, apparently Facebook thought it was a good idea to post on my behalf. The majority of my notifications and messages are from people I haven't talked to in years wondering what happened. Following Logan's advice, I change my photo to my old default image and log out.

"Heart emoji, shocked emoji, smiley face." He talks out loud as his fingers work over the keyboard. "Dinner?"

"What are you doing?" I chuckle at hearing the word emoji come out of his mouth.

"Commenting on your new profile picture."

"No, you're not." Sitting up on my knees, I look over his shoulder.

Sure enough, he commented asking me to dinner.

His head lulls to the side, blue eyes find mine, "I'm sorry for hurting your feelings before, was never my intent."

"It's alright." I shrug, "I'm sorry for acting like a brat and then not even thanking you."

"It's alright." He echoes, smiling at me. "Does this mean you're ready to get back to work?"

"What's the point? He's with Monica, you saw for yourself."

"He won't even remember her name when I'm done with you."

I roll my eyes, "Why do you care?" It's an honest question. I'm a nobody while he's a somebody, I'm plain while he's gorgeous, it makes no sense.

"You're my pet project." He smiles, "Plus, I've got a bet to win, remember?"

I give a defeated laugh, "The odds aren't exactly in your favor."

"Sure they are."

"If you say so."

"So what do you say, Duckie?"

"Duckie?"

"I'm trying something new."

I shake my head and laugh, "I don't like it."

"I know. So what'll it be?"

I don't understand his dedication to this, but he's kind of grown on me over the last eight weeks. And though he can be a total asshole at times, he also has the ability to be charming

150

when he wants to be. after all is said and done, I may not have Cole back, but at least I'll have a friend.

"When do we start?"

CHAPTER SEVENTEEN

Sitting in my usual chair at Logan's the following week, I'm about ready to kill him. With my new wardrobe up to his standards, he needed something new to insult. Today, it's my hair. He greeted me by calling me, Raggedy Ann. Which isn't so bad, but then he added that I looked like Raggedy Ann if she got her hair stuck in a vacuum after spending the afternoon with a toddler and a pair of scissors.

Apparently, air drying your hair is a criminal offense to the wealthy.

"How often do you shave?"

"I don't know. Couple times a month maybe." His face contorts in disgust as he stares at my jean-clad legs, "What? I'm always in pants, plus you can't really see it anyway."

"Not the point," He whines, his face still soured, "You can feel it." He gives an exaggerated shiver, "Women are supposed to be soft, not rival their men for hairiest legs."

Setting the expo marker on the counter, he moves over to take his seat. "Please tell me your armpits get more attention."

Raising my arms, I pull the sleeve of my t-shirt lower to display my hairless pits. "Every day."

"Thank God, I was afraid there for a moment." Shaking his head, he leans back pointing to my pants, "What's that area like?"

After a moment it dawns on me that it's not my pants he's pointing to, "That's not even close to being your business!" I shriek.

"You're here to learn the art of dating. Dating means eventually having sex, sex and grooming habits go hand in hand, therefore, making it my business. And I'll go ahead and say this now; no man wants to fuck Chewbacca."

"Oh my God, we're not talking about this." Heat creeps up my neck.

"How bad is it?"

"Logan, no."

"Its full cavewoman style isn't it?"

"Logan!"

"What?"

"Next topic."

"You know you're going to have to clean up your furburger, right?"

"That's disgusting."

"If he has to floss after going down on you; there's a problem."

"Oh, ew! For the love of God, it's not like that, thank you very much. And I'm not after some guy, I'm after Cole, and he doesn't do that, so I don't see that being a problem. Next topic."

His face contorts in disbelief, "What do you mean he doesn't do that?"

"Exactly what I said, next topic."

"This is the next topic."

"Okay, then pass."

"No passing. He doesn't period or just not regularly?"

"The details of my sex life aren't up for conversation."

"I was hoping what you lacked in personality you'd make up in bed, but it appears you're just as boring there too."

"You're an asshole; I happen to have both personality and a surprisingly interesting sex life."

"Then surprise me." He challenges, "Name one thing you do sexually that's interesting.

Leaving your clothes on during missionary doesn't count."

Fearing my cheeks are about to catch fire, I look away from him, crossing my arms over my chest, "This isn't any of your business."

"You're mumbling."

"I said, it's none of your business."

"The more you talk about Cal, the less I understand your affections towards him."

"His name is Cole. C-O-L-E, Cole."

"What kind of name is that anyway?"

"One with letters in it. Are we going to get to the point of today or not?"

"If it wasn't obvious already, today's topic is hair." With that, he pulls a cardboard box from one of the stools lining his kitchen island and places it in my lap.

Opening it, I find maybe sixteen or seventeen bottles of stuff. "I'm confused." I look up at him.

"Your homework is to use one product a day. I know you're not a fan of spending a lot of time on your appearance," His hand waves over me in an 'obviously' kind of way. "So, each product in there is for minimal maintenance, read the instructions and try them."

"What's the point?" I ask pulling a golden bottle out of the box; I draw it to my nose, oh that smells nice.

"Because men like hair. We like touching it, smelling it, and fantasizing about it. That mess you have checks none of those boxes."

"Fantasizing? What kind of messed up fetishes are you into?"

"It's not a fetish; we like picturing it wrapped around our fist while we're nailing a girl from behind, imagining it against our thighs or splayed out across our pillows."

I know my face is scrunched up, but I can't seem to unscrew it, "Kay."

Setting the bottle back into the box, I move everything to the floor at my feet.

"Don't be a prude." He scolds, "Sex is a big deal, you're not fifteen anymore. People fuck, some dirtier than others, but everyone does it."

"It's not that I'm a prude, it's just now every time I use one of these I'm going to be thinking that the goal is to have some guy fantasize about it."

"It's not like we walk down the street and imagine those things with every woman who walks by." He laughs, "Once you know the person and begin exploring how you feel about her, that's when that comes into play."

"Yeah until I get a compliment and it's all I'm able to think about."

"A compliment is aiming a little high don't you think? Let's keep this realistic."

I laugh, throwing a weak kick in his direction, "You're such a dick."

"But I get results. Trust me."

Surprisingly, I think I do trust him.

CHAPTER EIGHTEEN

Walking into Logan's house the following week, I twirl in a circle, showing off the new outfit I got. I'm in a black skater skirt with a daisy patterned shirt framed with a denim jacket. I even went so far as to wear black stockings and tall boots.

"You having a seizure?"

Stopping dead in my twirl I glare at him. "I bought this today, all by myself. I was thinking about wearing it this weekend for my birthday."

He nods casually, "You should."

"Yeah?" I smile wide, thankful for some form of approval.

"Sure. What product are you testing today?" He asks, referring to my hair.

"It's that same one as yesterday." I chew on my lip, "I know you want me to try them all, but I really like this one." It's a Wonder Wave spray; I just spritz my hair when it's damp, and it pulls my natural waves forward, giving me a similar look to beach waves.

"If you're happy with it you don't have to use the others."

My smile grows, "You're awfully nice today."

"You said it was your birthday." He shrugs it off.

"Not that I want you to stop being nice," I start, moving to take my chair, "but my birthday's this weekend, not today."

"Same difference."

I'm not even going to attempt to correct that; if he wants to be kind to me then I'm not going to complain, "So now that I have a hairstyle, clothes, and enough sitting and talking practice to last me a lifetime, are we moving up to T?"

He laughs like I made a joke, "No, we've made progress, but we're not finished."

"Ugh, what's left?"

"I was going to wait, but I supposed today seems as good a day as any. Get your purse; we're going on a field trip."

THE ART OF DATING

Our field trip landed me in a salon chair. This is my 'Birthday present' from Logan. I'm not going to argue, I've always wanted a change, just never had any good ideas. I'm equal parts nervous and excited as the attendant asks what I want. Seeing as the closest I get to pampering is box dye, I tell her I don't have a clue just that I have a hair product that I love and whatever style she chooses needs to be low maintenance. She gives me a confident nod and begins running her fingers through my curls.

After a moment to herself, she dedicates the next hour to dousing my hair with sour chemicals, then wrapping my head, bangs to neck in tinfoil. I dare any alien who opposes me to come forward now; he doesn't stand a chance at brain scrambling with this much aluminum.

The stylist is polite; she asks about my job, nodding and laughing along when I get a little too into the conversation about my favorite books, even asks for recommendations when she moves me to the sink.

The potency of the dye burns my nose when the foil is pulled from each section before being chased away by a heavenly floral shampoo. A head massage and rinse later I'm back in the chair.

At this point, I'm not sure if my hammering heart is from fear or joy when her scissors start snipping along the edges of my hair, she never did tell me what she was planning.

I watch her reflection with great interest; the swipe of the white comb, the beat of her scissors cutting into my wet hair.

When the scissors are replaced with a hair dryer I'm pleased with the lack of length she removed, my hair still falls just below my shoulders, but now I have multiple layers, creating a full and styled look rather than that lioness thing I usually have going on.

My hair begins to lighten under the dryer, thin honey lines appear next to chestnut locks, transforming my dull mousy hair into walkway model brown. I thoroughly love this.

I love it more when a woman opens a black trunk next to me, filled with every color polish and filing implements known to man. I choose a neutral shade and hand over my hand willingly as the next attendant approaches me with a tray of makeup. I have never been so spoiled in my life, and I'm giddy over it. So giddy in fact I welcome the idea of makeup, allowing her to demonstrate each product on the back of her

161

hand before applying in thin, even coverage. I look like a fucking model; it's a shame my birthday isn't until this weekend because I feel like strutting myself everywhere right now.

CHAPTER NINETEEN

When I'm finally released I smile at my flawless reflection before skipping over to Logan who waits in a leather chair; a magazine is draped over his knee and ankle.

"So?" I ask, wearing the smile that refuses to leave.

He blinks hard, "Wow." My smile grows to the point of pain. "Very nice."

Collecting his magazine from his lap, he drops it onto the table at his side before standing.

"Thank you for this."

"Of course."

I walk with him to the register running my hair through my silky locks.

"I take it you're pretty happy?" He asks, handing the woman a black card.

"Very much so."

"Good, cause there's one more thing. Thank you," He says to the attendant before turning back to me.

"What's that?" What's left is what I should have said.

He doesn't reply, simply smiles and nods to an angry looking granny in an apron.

I watch her approach like she's about to eat my soul.

"She's ready." He tells her, his hand landing on my lower back, inching me forward.

"Ready for what?"

"We wax." She says in a heavy German accent.

Remember that smile that wouldn't go away? It's gone, wiped from my face as horror takes over.

"What?!" I shriek, taking a step back.

He catches my arm, jerking me forward. "Brazilian."

"Absolutely not." I shake my head.

"Ignore her, First-time jitters."

"More like fuck-you jitters, I'm not doing that."

"This way." She instructs, walking away.

164

"No, thank you."

She reminds me of one of those teachers with a ruler and disdain for children.

"Now." She orders, walking through a door, I can see the bed from my spot next to Logan.

"Not happening," I turn on Logan.

"Do you want Chris back, yes or no?"

I scrunch my face up with a whine, "Yes, and it's Cole."

"Then get your ass in that room and clean that shit up, it's a fire hazard."

"I don't want to."

"Too bad. He's gotta be able to find it to fuck it."

"Gross. You're such a dick." I grumble, shouldering past him.

Entering into the small room my adrenaline has my heart racing, why did I come in here? I don't want to do this, and I especially don't want to do it with her.

"Use the wipe to clean the area; then you'll remove your lower clothing and lay down with the towel over your waist." Removing a towel from a cabinet, she sets it on top of the bed with a packet before leaving.

With shaky fingers, I kick out of my shoes while reaching under my skirt to hook my stockings and underwear then draw them down

165

my legs. Grabbing the little packet from the bed, I put my back to the door in case she comes barging in while my ass is hanging out, and pull the wipe from its sleeve. I jerk at the chill of the pad while thoroughly cleaning every nook and cranny I can find, more out of nerves than cleanliness.

Depositing it into the trash, I lay stiffly on the bed. Folding my skirt onto my stomach, I seek the barely-there modesty of the towel. I might puke while laying here waiting for Hitler to waltz back in.

As if sensing my thoughts, the door opens. She doesn't speak nor look in my direction when she comes in, simply shuts the door and starts to stir the little cylinder of wax.

She spins around abruptly, popping the back of my hand with hers. I withdraw at the strike and stare at her in shock; she is no-nonsense as she whips the towel to my chest, immediately spreading hot goo all over my crotch.

"Breathe." She instructs.

I inhale before the worst pain in existence takes over.

"MARY MOTHER OF CHRIST." I cry, trying to close my legs.

THE ART OF DATING

Broom Hilda will not be shaken that easily. She spears one of her boney elbows into my knee, forcing it down while the other hand smears the wax over the other side. She's surprisingly strong for being so little. Another agonizing rip.

"FUCK! What did I ever do to you?!"

I swear to the man above the corner of her mouth just rose. She looks like the type to enjoy watching others suffer. I bet she's one of those Madam's who dresses her man up as a dog.

Throwing my head back I grunt and grit my teeth as another rip sounds in the room.

Pull after pull she goes, at this point I'm convinced she's just ripping the entire thing off.

FINALLY, she smears oil over my burning bits, I blow out a tortured breath, too scared to look down at what I'm sure is the bloody remains of my vagina.

"Roll on your side."

"For what?" I ask as she tries to twist my body.

"For the backside."

"The backside of what?!" My eyes just might fall out of my head.

"The backside." She slaps my thigh, and I bat away her hands, "Stop hitting me!"

She puts her hands on her hips, "Roll over."

167

"The backside of what?"

"*Your* backside."

"You want to wax my ass?" She nods curtly, "FUCK. NO."

"Mr. Devitt said full wax."

"Mr. Devitt can go fly a kite," I say wrapping the towel around my waist, sitting up. "Wax my ass, are you kidding me? WHY? Why would anyone do that?"

She glares at me, refusing to answer.

Hobbling off the table, I open the door to see Logan seated in one of the fancy leather chairs again, he looks up and starts laughing, "My ass?!" I yell across the room.

He laughs harder, hiding his smile under his hand.

"How about you get in here and wax yours, huh? I'm sure Hitler's mom would love that."

"Just do it." He tries to sound stern, but he's still laughing.

"No! Why would anyone need to do that?"

"For a few reasons, none of which I'm sure you want to discuss while in a busy establishment.

For the first time, I realize everyone is staring at me. My cheeks burn as I slowly recoil back into the room.

"Lay down."

"Fuck you, Adolph." Grabbing my clothing off the counter, I start to put them on while keeping my eyes trained on the horrible little Nazi. My crotch roars against the scratch of fabric.

Once they're up, I throw the towel on the bed and sidestep the still angry troll woman.

Throwing the door open, I glare at Logan, "You're on my shitlist!"

"Language." He scolds, still trying to calm his smile. "It's not ladylike."

"Fuck your ladylike bullshit. I just got my soul ripped out of my hair follicles. You and I," I point between our chests, "Not friends right now."

"What if I buy you a cookie?"

I stop and glare, "If by cookie you mean a new vagina that doesn't burn like the devil himself just went down on me, sure then we could be friends."

"Two cookies?" He shows me two fingers, "Two big cookies."

"Is that an innuendo?"

"Nope."

"They better be the best damn cookies of my life."

CHAPTER TWENTY

My vagina eventually stopped burning. I'm sure it was quite a sight for Amy when she came home Tuesday to see me laying on the couch with a bag of ice pressed between my legs. Of course, she had a good laugh at my expense when I told her I was ready to hit the streets looking like the pretty penny I'm sure Logan spent before what I'm naming as, 'the event,' happened. Instead, my night was spend icing my crotch and eating cookies.

"HAPPY BIRTHDAY!" Amy squeals, rushing out of her bedroom to lay on top of me.

I grunt under her weight. "Thanks,"

"Are you going to Logan's today?" She asks, rolling off me.

"No, he's out of town until Monday."

"So what are you going to do today?"

"Edit probably. With all the time I spend with Logan, I keep falling behind."

"That sounds boring; you're not supposed to work on your birthday."

"You've gotta work, Logan's working, oh look, I'm all out of friends to spend the day with."

"What about Vanessa or James?"

"Those are your friends."

"Our friends."

"Sure, sure. I know them through you, but I've never hung out with them or anyone else when you weren't there."

"That's because you're some hermit that spends her birthdays working."

I shrug, hoisting myself off the pull out before offering her my hand.

Drawing her upright, I jerk forward when she swats my butt, "Jerk."

"I only work until eight so be ready when I get home so we can go to dinner."

I nod, producing an obnoxious yawn.

"You talk to your mom yet?" She asks, poking her head into the fridge.

"Yeah, her and my dad called earlier. I also got a text from your parents; they sent me flowers. Should be here later today."

171

"They never send me flowers." She whines.

"Nope, just rent money." I tease. Her response is to throw a cup of yogurt at me.

Laughing, I set it on the counter separating the kitchen from the living room.

"I'm going to go shower."

"Dress cute tonight, please?"

"I planned on wearing that skirt with the denim jacket, is that okay?"

"Yeah, that works. Oh, hey, is it okay if I invite people to go out with us?"

I shrug, "I don't care."

"Cool, the more people we invite, the more free booze you get."

Valid. Though I'm not a big drinker, I can usually sneak it to Amy who loves alcohol.

Wishing her a good day, I slip into the bathroom.

Quarter to nine, my hair's done, makeup's on, and I'm fully dressed scrolling through Facebook, thanking people for their birthday wishes when Amy comes in.

"Hey," She starts, shutting the door, "Sorry. It took forever to get a cab."

"It's okay." I smile, "Take your time; we have all night."

"How'd work go?" She asks from the belly of her bedroom.

"Good. Finished one of the books I was working on and got started on another. What about you?"

She scoffs, "Hell. Apparently, when you do your job right, you get to do everyone else's too. I swear I hate people."

I smile, looking down at the laptop. Scrolling down, I see Logan's comment on my photo. Out of morbid curiosity, I click on his profile.

His profile picture is of him on a boat; he's wearing a pair of aviators, a black tee, and swim trunks. It's stupid how he can still look good with no effort.

Clicking through his photo, I notice a woman, equally as beautiful as him, appears in more than one image. She's got stunning blue eyes and platinum blonde hair; everything about her screams wealthy. They look like the perfect match, I wonder who she is, not that I'll ever ask, but I am curious. Looking through the comments and likes, I try to find her profile, but nothing comes of my search.

"Ready?"

"Look at this girl," I angle the screen at Amy.

"Who is she?"

"I don't know. She's in a bunch of pictures with Logan though."

"Has he mentioned a girlfriend or anything?" I shake my head, "Maybe she's an ex."

"Maybe. She's pretty though, isn't she?"

She shrugs, "I guess."

I know damn well Amy thinks she's just as pretty as I do, but Amy's petty and will disregard anyone who isn't me when it comes to Logan; she seems to believe we're destined for one another, her words not mine.

Setting my computer down, I get up to meet her at the door.

"Where to, birthday girl?"

After eating at my favorite burger joint, we walk hand in hand down the streets of Lenox Hill. Every few feet, she extends her phone for 'birthday selfies' as she calls them.

"At this rate, we're never going to get to the bar," I tell her, smiling broadly for the photo.

Lowering the phone, she looks over the image, "It's just up here."

"Up where?" I look around, "These are all expensive up here."

"Not where we're going."

174

I think her information might be bad, but I don't tell her that. This is my old neighborhood, if there were a cheap bar close by I'd have known about it, the only places I know of are clubs with cover charges.

"See?" She waves at a building to our right.

"All I see is Royals," I admit, trying to find the secret hole in the wall bar she must be pointing to.

"That's it."

I stop, halting her with me, "We can't afford this place. It's like a hundred bucks a person."

"Not tonight it's not." She says jerking her arm forward, so I stumble after her.

"Look at the line," I nod to the sea of people crowding the sidewalk, "Even if we could afford it, it's not like we'd ever get in."

"Trust me." She says shimming up to the doorman. I don't think this is going to work out the way she wants it to. "Hi, Amy Marshal and Devina Anderson."

Raising the board at his hip, he looks over his list. I'm shocked when he nods us through.

"Whoa, seriously?"

"I told you." She smiles, looping her arm through mine.

Walking inside, music blares from overhead speakers. Multicolored lights bounce off the

175

walls reminding me of a rave. Everything is high end and chic looking. Following the crowd to the bar area, I'm redirected to the left. "Wait, isn't the club that way?" I point over my shoulder.

"Yeah, but we're not going there."

"Where are we going?"

"You'll see."

I follow her up a set of stairs, passing by a sign that reads, VIP ONLY.

"What have you done?" I yell over the music.

"Managed to keep my mouth shut." She smiles.

"What does that mean?"

She doesn't have the opportunity to answer before a group of familiar faces smile back at me from a private bar.

CHAPTER TWENTY-ONE

All at once everyone starts singing Happy Birthday at the top of their lungs. Amy pushes me forward to the center of the group; I'm surprised to see Logan among the many faces, leaning casually against the bar, he too sings along.

I'm passed around to all of Amy, and I's mutual friends, showered with birthday wishes and hugs, the last being Logan.

"I thought you were out of town?" I say, wrapping my arms around his waist in a quick embrace.

"I lied."

"Clearly." I smile, "So I take it I have you to thank for the location?"

"And the free booze!" Amy says, handing me a shot glass.

Looking up from my glass, I met his blue eyes. "Really?" He nods, picking up his glass of amber liquid. Warmth blooms in my chest at his generosity, "Thank you."

"Who's going to toast?" Amy asks, her eyes searching to make sure everyone has a glass.

"I'll do it." Logan volunteers, raising his tumbler. Masking my surprise, I raise my glass with everyone else, "To Devina! You don't look a day over forty-two." I roll my eyes, joining in the surrounding laughter. "Happy Birthday, Duck."

"To Duck!" They all chorus, making me laugh at their use of his less than appealing nickname for me.

After everyone's glass clinks against mine, we throw them back in unison, the bitter sting of the tequila coats my throat with a hotline.

Amy woos, dropping her empty glass on the bar, "Let's dance!"

"I'm going to need more alcohol before that happens." Logan's brow quirks, "You too if you're going to be witness to it."

Leaning over the bar, Logan orders us another round, giving me a double this time. I can already tell tomorrow's going to suck when

I down the double in record speed, my head warms immediately; oh yeah, definitely going suck. Not being a big fan of alcohol, I'm an extreme lightweight. But you only turn twenty-eight once, so fuck it.

This time when Amy reaches for my hand, I let her take it. Her hips are gyrating before we even reach the dance floor. You know you're 'that girl' when three shots have you buzzing hard enough you think you're the next winner of, *So you think you can dance*.

My hips sway to the music, my arms raised high above my head, allowing the alcohol to take the wheel for a while. I'm in that sweet spot of drinking; lose, free, and completely uncaring to the world around me. Giddy with booze and music, and I let them both run wild through my veins.

Amy sways closer, locking her fingers between mine, I'm spun around in circles, the club blurring into a sea of lines, just as my head starts to fog, I'm twirled back into a rock-hard chest. Air expels from my lungs in a rush, as I draw my first breath; it's thick with the familiar sporty scent of Logan.

He smiles a brilliant smile, "Look at you, all carefree and beautiful."

179

"I thought I was the forty-year-old ugly duck." I tease, letting him draw me into his hips.

"Yeah, well, you're so ugly you're cute."

Smiling off his jab, I close my eyes, soaking up the heat of the room, the rhythm of the music, and the strong arms around me.

My high is interrupted by a blonde, balancing four shot glasses. "Bottom's up, girlie."

Taking two of them, we swallow in quick succession. After handing them back to her, I fall into Logan once again, "I haven't drank this much in a couple of years." I admit, "I don't know what kind of drunk I am, so I apologize in advance."

"It's your birthday; you can puke if you want to."

"On you, if I can get my aim right." He shrugs, the right side of his mouth tipping up, "Why are you being so nice to me?"

"It's your birthday. Plus I like this side of you."

"And what's so different?"

"You haven't stopped smiling since we got here."

"Shut up," I scold, "I smile."

"Not like this." He shakes his head, his face growing serious, "You don't have a care in the world do you?"

"Nope." I giggle when he spins me again, though he takes mercy on me and only does it once before pulling me flush against him.

The sober part of me warns that I'm too close, that we're too close, but the alcohol quickly shoves sober me into a dark corner and embraces the moment.

I don't know how long we dance for but by the time Amy pulls us all back to the bar I'm covered in a fine layer of sweat and my heart is beating almost as fast as the techno number blaring from the overhead speakers.

"My turn!" Amy announces with an angelic smile, she raises her glass high, "I've known this bitch for *twenty-four years*. She's cuddled me when I've been upset, held my hair when I was drunk and has been there at every turn in my life, cheering me on like a crazy person. We've fought, shared our most guarded secrets, and driven each other to the point of insanity. But if there's anyone on this earth that I would want to be crazy with, it's this bombshell right here. To twenty-four years of memories, twenty-four years of sisterhood, and twenty-four years of having the greatest best friend this world has ever seen! I love you with all my heart, Happy Birthday, Dee!"

Amy clinks her glass on mine before kissing me square on the mouth in her timeless tradition of 'Birthday Kisses,' the others follow suit, tapping my glass with theirs before pecking me on the lips. This is old news to me; it's been the norm for so long that it's never been awkward or uncomfortable; until now.

Time slows down entirely while butterflies rage war. Logan gently knocks his tumbler against mine, the side of his mouth tipping up. My heart beats out of control as his fingers snake around my neck, gently tipping my head back,

And.

The.

World.

Stops.

His lips press against mine, soft and firm, molding perfectly around me for what feels like an eternity before pulling away, his fingers lingering just a moment too long. It's like a cliffhanger at the end of a really good book, you're floored by how great it was, but at the same time, you feel disappointment that's it over and physically ache to continue.

Drawing my bottom lip nervously between my teeth, I note the bourbon lingering on my skin. I know it only lasted a fraction of a second, but it feels so much longer.

"To Devina!" Amy shouts, utterly unfazed by what just happened.

Lazily lifting my glass, I sneak a peek at Logan before erasing the taste of his drink with mine.

CHAPTER TWENTY-TWO

"Ah!" Amy shrieks, "No!" Bending low, she attempts to pick up one of her heels that slipped out of her drunken fingers; it dances across the sidewalk before she finally manages to grab the ankle strap. "I just dropped my Valentino Garavani's on the ground!" She whines into her Snapchat story.

Logan has his arm draped over my shoulder as we walk back to the apartment. I know he has a car we could have taken, but I don't remember why we chose to walk instead.

It's almost four in the morning, and we're all trashed. I think Logan's even a little drunk; we're both guilty of being a little touch-friendly tonight. Searching my alcohol-induced thoughts, I try to remember a moment where one of us wasn't touching the other in one way or another but come up empty.

I'm too drunk to care; I was too drunk to care after shot four, to be honest. He smells good and has strong arms, not to mention he's gorgeous.

"How are you feeling, Dee?" She asks, still holding up her phone.

"Intoxicated." I laugh, leaning into Logan's ribs for support.

Reaching up, I pull his jacket tighter around my shoulders. It must be freezing if I'm able to feel the chill of the night with this much booze running through my system.

"Home sweet home." Amy sighs, pulling the lobby door open. Logan catches it and holds it open for me.

Amy's taking the stairs like a pro while the first step almost sends me falling on my ass.

"Whoa," I sway feeling like I weigh about a hundred pounds too much, a firm hand lands on my lower back. "I don't remember these stairs being quite this daunting, or angled."

Logan laughs, raising a fist in the air, "Have no fear, the millionaire's here!"

Taking my arm, he throws it over his shoulder, twisting, so his back is against my front. Bending low, he hooks his fingers behind my knees and lifts me onto his back. I squeal with delight, squeezing his neck in fear of falling while the room spins in multiple directions.

Amy laughs running up the stairs in front of us, shoes in one hand, cell phone in the other, "Ahhh!" She yells into the screen before angling it over her shoulder, "Say hi to Snapchat!"

"Hi!" Logan and I sing at once, both laughing like idiots.

"Oh em gee, aren't they freaking adorable?!" She whines into the screen. A second later I hear our laughter echoing out of her phone.

Running across the landing, she sprints halfway up the next flight before turning abruptly, using the wall to steady her intoxicated body, "Say cheese!"

Shaking my head to remove the hair from my face, I grin like an idiot over Logan's shoulder, "Cheeeeese."

Amy laughs, typing on her phone.

Finally making it to the fourth floor, Logan lets me slide off his back. The hall spins as Amy unlocks the door, throwing her shoes across the room upon entry. And to think she was just screaming about how she dropped one.

"I don't want tonight to end." She says, spinning in fast circles, arms wide. Losing balance, she falls to the floor in a heap of laughter.

Logan must've closed the door behind himself because when I turn to do it, I find it already shut.

"Ugh, tonight was fun." I hear the slur in my words but don't attempt to correct it.

"Ames, help me get the couch out," I say, stumbling forward. I grab one of the cushions and throw it at the useless heap of a best friend still cackling on the floor.

I'm surprised when a pair of hands appear in front of me, removing the middle seat, oh yeah, Logan's here. After pulling the coffee table to the side, he pulls the mattress out effortlessly, that usually takes me two or three tries and here he is showing me up.

I waste no time climbing into the center of my bed, oh this feels like heaven.

"You better not be going to sleep," Amy growls, crawling onto the mattress.

"I'm not," I mumble, my hand fumbling over the contents of the table until I find the remote.

"Come on, Logan." She reaches forward, taking his hand and pulls him forward. "Every year we watch Breakfast at Tiffany's together. You're my plus one."

My body's an anvil as I try to pull my dead limbs upright to make room for him. He sits against the back of the couch next to me, his long legs crossed at the ankle while Amy lays at our feet, attempting to get the DVD onto the tray without having to get up.

After a few tries, she succeeds, collapsing into the mattress, "How come we never think to put the disc in before we get drunk?"

"And miss all that?" Logan asks with a laugh. "I hope you never remember."

"Don't jinx us," I whine, trying to focus my eyes long enough to skip forward to the menu. I feel like an owl; eyes wide after exaggerated blinks just for a half-second of clarity. Finally, I find the right button and start the movie.

"I want a poor slob without a name." Amy cries, staring longingly at the screen.

"A what?" Logan asks in genuine confusion.

"That's what Holly calls the cat in this movie." I answer for her, "She's allergic to them though so she can't have one."

He gives a heavy nod; I don't think I'm the only one who feels like they weigh too much.

Sinking lower, I feel the dryness of my eyes and the pull of peaceful surrender; I make it

until Paul steps out of the cab before my eyes
seal shut.

THE ART OF DATING

LOGAN

I have the most beautiful woman in existence in my arms right now. Her hair spilled across my chest in brown waves, her tight little body folded into my ribs, her legs tangled around mine, I'm in heaven. Well, except for the raging hard-on. Very, very slowly I free my hand from under her arm, adjusting my dick to be less obvious before pulling my phone out of my pocket. Searching for nearby restaurants, I find one with a to-go menu and order us all a greasy breakfast of eggs, bacon, and bagels before forwarding the order to Caleb.

ME: Can you bring this to Devina's apartment, please. The girls are still asleep so don't knock. Message me, and I'll come open the door.

THE ART OF DATING

CALEB: ETA 15 min.

Setting my phone on the arm of the couch, my fingers idly run through her hair. Last night was easily the best night of my life; it was better than losing my virginity, greater than seeing my name engraved above the headquarters' doors, and destroyed the night in Cancun after graduation. Seeing Devina so carefree and radiant stole all of those moments. She really has no clue how beautiful she is, you'd think a mirror would be enough but man...ugh, she's breathtaking, and I wish she'd just see it already.

Her hand squeezes tighter around my ribs, her hips slightly grinding against my leg. What I wouldn't give for her friend to be anywhere but at our feet right now. I'd add a little pressure and watch her come alive, the second her eyes would open I'd roll her over, kissing her tequila flavored lips until neither of us had any air left in our lungs. My hands would rid her of her clothing, my mouth memorizing every dip and curve of her body until she was begging for me. I'd give her everything that needle dick prick doesn't; I'd fuck her until she was mine, wipe out every thought, no, the very existence of him from her mind. Treat her the way she deserves to be treated.

191

THE ART OF DATING

A soft hum escapes her lips pulling my thoughts to reality. Oh hell, I'm going to snap my zipper in half if I don't get my thoughts together, all she has to do is open her eyes, and my dick would be the first thing she'd see. On second thought... no, no, too much. She's blinded by the idea she wants that bastard and seeing my junk is sure to push her away.

My phone vibrates with a message from Caleb; I don't need to read it to know he's outside her door. Adjusting my hard-on for the second time, I turn to face the gorgeous creature in my arms. It's almost painful to wake her, but if she continues to nuzzle into me like this, I'm going to end up ruining everything, and it's entirely too early in the plan to deviate now.

CHAPTER TWENTY-THREE

I wake up to my bed jerking underneath me.

A male voice whispers while fingers gently run through my hair, "Hey, pretty girl."

It sounds a lot like Logan, but that's crazy cause Logan wouldn't be in my- oh my God. My eyes shoot open,

He smiles when my shocked eyes land on him. "You drool."

"I do not." Oh hell, my head hurts.

"Sure you do, that's how I know you were dreaming about me."

"I'll kill both of you if you don't stop talking."

THE ART OF DATING

Looking down at the foot of the bed, I see Amy sprawled out at our feet. I say our feet because the way I'm wrapped around Logan, it's hard to tell whose limb belongs to who.

Quickly untangling myself, I mumble an apology while rolling over to my side of the bed.

"How are you holding up?" I ask the lump known as Amy to avoid looking at Logan.

"Miserable. What about you?"

"A little better than you." My choice to avoid looking at Logan is void by curiosity as he sits up, his hand openly adjusting himself while he stands, making a b-line for the front door.

"Thank you." He says, opening the door, "I'll call when I'm ready."

I hear a male murmur from the other side before he closes the door, in his hands is a blue box.

"Is someone here?" Amy drawls against the mattress.

"I had Caleb bring the cure for hangovers," Logan says from the counter.

Opening the box, the scent of greasy breakfast food fills the room, turning my stomach. I'm not the only one, Amy forces her nose into the blanket while groaning. "That's going to make me puke."

"Me too, take it away."

"My God." Logan stares at me, "Did you just turn down food?"

"I'm pretty sure I drank half the bar last night," I groan while my stomach churns.

"It works, I promise." He says holding a plate out to me.

"I don't want it." I mock cry. "I'm gonna puke."

He sets the plate down on the mattress beside me, just seeing the pile of scrambled eggs is enough to make me gag.

Wrapping my hand around my mouth, I skyrocket off the mattress and into the bathroom, dry heaving over the toilet. I hear Logan laugh as he approaches the still open door, "You need something to throw up."

"Fuck off, Logan."

Hearing the tap turn on, the tell-tale sound of a glass filling with water sounds as I continue to dry heave. He sets the glass of water next to me on the floor and leaves, closing the door as he goes.

Knowing he has a point, I take the glass and drown myself in the tepid liquid, moving the cup just in time to empty my stomach.

Oh, this is miserable, now that I've started I can't stop.

THE ART OF DATING

"I'm dying," I yell through the door, resting my cheek on the cold plastic seat.

After managing to keep a glass of tap water down, I scrub my face and arms with cold water. This is why I don't drink, sure it's a blast while you're out but the day after is always the same.

"Where's your toaster?" Logan asks Amy when I come out of the restroom.

"I left it at Devina's apartment."

"You have an apartment?" He asks as I climb back onto the bed.

I shake my head, "No, it's Cole's."

"That she's still paying rent for."

"Amy!" I scold, kicking her bare foot.

"Well, you are."

"Shut up."

"You're paying rent on an apartment you're not even living in?"

"I haven't taken my name off the lease yet; I keep forgetting."

"She thinks if she kicks him out he'll never come back."

"You're so much prettier with your mouth *shut*."

"Wait," Logan says, stepping out from behind the counter. "You said he was living with that girl." I nod, "So you're paying for your ex-boyfriend and his mistress to live together?"

"I'm not paying for them to live together." I defend, picking at a piece of egg, "I just forgot to inform the office I'm no longer there."

"Why haven't you just called them?" He presses further.

"I don't know." I say in agitation, "Probably because it's a great apartment and the rent isn't crippling. If he moves out, I could lose it."

"I keep telling her to kick him out; he's not even on the lease."

I glare at Amy while Logan takes her side, "I agree, it's your apartment."

"Well, your goal here is to get us back together, so what's the point of kicking him out if he's just going to move back in?"

"Because you're paying for it." He says almost appalled, "None of this is going to work if he thinks he can have you back at a drop of a hat."

"But..." I say slowly, "He can."

"Men want what they can't have."

"You must be dying when you're around me then." Amy mumbles.

"Every day." He smiles in her direction.

A nasty feeling blooms in my stomach, I feel almost jealous. But that's preposterous; I want

Logan, I've always wanted Logan- Shit, I mean, Cole. Wide-eyed, I glance up at him like he might have heard my thoughts. He's in the room, I probably just replaced Cole's name because he's here.

Tipping my head down, I avoid looking at him as I push my food around my plate. My nausea has more or less passed, but I still don't have much of an appetite.

"You know I'm going to have to rectify this right?" Logan says from the kitchen.

I look up at him, "Rectify what?"

"Him living there. First, we're going to need to work on your seduction skills."

My face scrunches up, "Why?"

"Because I need you to be alluring and uninterested, not stare at him like a love-struck puppy."

"Who says I can't be alluring and uninterested?"

Amy chuckles while Logan gives me an incredulous glare.

"What?"

"Fine," He says standing, "Show me what you've got."

"On who? You?" He nods, "I'm not going to flirt with you."

"Come on, don't be a wuss."

"I'll do it." Amy volunteers with a laugh, though she refuses to get up after saying it.

"What's the worst that can happen?" He smiles at me.

"You could fall in love with me." I tease, throwing a piece of egg in my mouth.

"Highly unlikely, have you seen the way you look in the morning?"

"Well, if you're that unimpressed with my bed head, you're more than welcome to crash at your own place." I smile sweetly at him.

"It was a little hard to get up and leave when I had a drunken heap laying on me."

I blush at the memory of me curled around him, "Could have just pushed me off."

He shrugs, "It was the only position you wouldn't snore in."

I sigh in annoyance, "I don't snore." Amy and Logan laugh at the same time, causing my cheeks to redden further. "I hate you both."

"It's not like you were calling the ships home or anything, though with the amount of spit dribbling out of your mouth I wouldn't be surprised if they were able to dock right here in your living room."

Amy laughs hard before groaning, her hands squeezing the sides of her head. "Ow,

199

shut up guys, I can't laugh right now, I think I'm still drunk."

"For your friend's sake, we'll get a raincheck on your flirting lesson."

"I don't need a raincheck or a lesson. I can manage just fine."

"Can you?"

Throwing my arms up from my lap, I growl. "Yes, Logan. I'm not completely worthless; I managed to get Cole didn't I? And let's not forget you asking me out."

"When?" He demands with a chuckle like the very idea is outrageous.

Jutting out my chin, I meet his humored eyes, "At that speed dating thing you asked me out, twice. Oh, and then the night of the masquerade."

"Correction, you asked me to dinner."

"Correction to your correction, I told you that you could tag along after I turned down your date."

He goes silent, his eyes unfocused as he tries to recall that night, "I think you might be right, I stand corrected."

"And don't you forget it either."

CHAPTER TWENTY-FOUR

"Stop fidgeting." Logan scolds for the third time since I learned about today's plan. Two and half weeks ago I admitted that Cole was living in my apartment, apparently that has to change.

We're currently in the elevator of my old apartment after Logan convinced the office aide to print an eviction notice. My heart pounds with nerves and guilt; my gut says this is a terrible idea.

"What's the plan?" He prompts for the second time.

"I'm to remain silent. If I'm spoken to, I smile politely and wait for you to reply. I'm not allowed to look at him like a love-struck puppy,

THE ART OF DATING

and if he isn't alone, I'm to pretend not to care."

He nods once, "Right. And what's the goal?"

"To appear indifferent."

"And why is that?"

"Because men want what they can't have," I answer just in time for the elevator to stop.

"Good girl. Here we go, ready?"

I chew on my lip, nodding and take the first step into the hall.

"Trust me." He says low, resting his hand on my lower back, "Which one is yours?" I point to the far left door, "Breathe."

Sucking in an exaggerated breath, I let him lead me in front of the door.

"Fix your face."

Shaking my head out, I push my shoulders back. "Ready."

Logan's fist comes down against the door in rapid, almost angry raps.

"I'm not ready," I say in a small panic.

Fingers wrap around mine, giving me a tight squeeze, "Yes, you are. Trust me."

The door pulls away from the frame to reveal the blonde skank. Logan releases my hand and offers it to her. "Hello, I'm Logan Devitt," pulling away, he opens the flap of the manila envelope and lifts the eviction note, "This is Devina

Anderson, we're here to talk to a," His eyes look over the paper, "Cole Hewitt." He eyes her expectantly when she doesn't answer right away.

"Like, Devitt Network, Logan Devitt?"

"In the flesh. Hewitt?"

"Oh, um. One sec."

Closing the door halfway, she calls for him over her shoulder. Taking a silent breath, I hold my features stoically in place as he opens the door, wearing nothing but a towel around his waist. Beads of water run down his chest, disappearing under the white fabric. Realizing I'm staring, I immediately lift my eyes to his.

"Devina?" My heart squeezes painfully; he only calls me by my name when he's mad. I smile, but it's saltier than I was aiming for. Looking me up and down, he rests his gray gaze on mine, "What are you doing here?"

"I'm Logan Devitt." Logan extends his hand forward once again.

"As in Devitt Network," Monica whispers, almost in a scold.

Peeling his eyes off mine, Cole gives her a passing look before shaking Logan's hand.

"Cole Hewitt."

"I'm well aware." Logan's tone is professional acid, his demeanor almost calling a smile to my lips. "Are you aware you aren't on the lease?"

"What?" Cole looks to me before giving Logan his attention.

"Yes, see this apartment is in Miss Anderson's name," Logan produces a sheet of paper from his envelope, handing it to him. "We have financial records of her continued payments here," Producing another sheet; he hands it over.

"What is this?" Cole asks me.

"And this," Logan goes on as if Cole never spoke, "Is an eviction notice. You have forty-eight hours to vacate the premise. Any personal belongings left in the dwelling after your allotted time will be considered forfeit of ownership."

"This is bullshit!" Cole seethes, fisting the documents in his hand, "This was *our* place, Dee."

"And now it's mine." I know I wasn't supposed to reply, but up until the eviction notice he wasn't able to take his eyes off me, cementing the fact that Logan's plan is working. It made me a little giddy.

"My lawyer is on standby if you have any questions or concerns," Logan tells him, handing over a business card.

Cole refuses to break eye contact with me, so Logan hands the card to Monica instead.

"We'll be refurnishing so don't be shy with the furniture." I smile, pulling away from the door. Logan's cheek twitches, following my lead. Once my back is to the door, a bright smile spreads across my face. I call the elevator, not even feeling the need to turn around.

"That was...empowering," I admit once the elevator doors close.

"You deviated." He scolds, but his tone isn't angry, it's more amused even if he's trying to hide it.

"Yeah, but I rocked the hell out of that situation."

"I agree." A smile finally blesses his face, "So, when will *we* be refurnishing?"

"Shut up," I laugh, "It just came out, plus it probably drove him crazy. Did you see the way he was staring at me?" Clasping my chest, I swoon against the wall of the elevator. "It's working."

"You should never doubt me." He smirks, stepping forward when the elevator doors open, "My plans always work."

CHAPTER TWENTY-FIVE

"Ew," Amy gags, "It smells like ass and gross pussy in here."

Huffing, I turn to glare at her. "Not funny."

"I wasn't trying to be." She admits, looking over my empty bedroom.

Cole managed to clear the majority of the apartment when he left yesterday. I'm left with the couch, my bookshelves, and an abundance of boxes containing all my stuff. I'm not sure what I was expecting to find, the idea of having my clothes still hanging from the closet, and toiletries still in their rightful place seems far-fetched and stupid, yet I was still surprised to find them thrown haphazardly into boxes and crammed into the closet.

THE ART OF DATING

I'm lucky to have Amy and Logan's help today, she assisted in packing up my belongings from her house and agreed to help me 'wash the stank' out of my apartment, whatever that means. Logan was our ride back and forth between Ames' apartment and the furniture store where I was able to acquire new furniture. I've been saving for a new apartment, now that I've reclaimed my old one, I had more than a pretty penny to splurge at the store.

"Oh, the guys are back." Amy claps, moving behind me.

"What are you so excited about?" I ask, picking up a box of books. "It's just Logan and Caleb."

"I know, but they're both wicked hot."

I scrunch my face, "Caleb's not hot, he's old."

"I prefer a Silver Fox." She winks.

"Are we talking about the same person?" I whisper, hearing Logan and Caleb talking down the hall, "Caleb doesn't have gray hair."

"Ugh, whatever, you're ruining my fun." She complains, walking out to join the guys with me in tow.

Emerging into the kitchen, Amy clears her throat, "Remember when you agreed that Logan's wicked hot?"

THE ART OF DATING

My face falls of any emotion while a burn unlike I've ever felt sinks into my cheeks. Caleb and Logan both stare at me while Amy sashays towards them, "I did not."

"Yes, you did. I said they were both wicked hot and you agreed that Logan was." She smiles a cocky grin over her shoulder. My options are to admit I think he's cute or have Amy out me that I said Caleb wasn't and hurt his feelings.

My eyes look to Logan who's got a smile that promises endless teasing. "It's alright," He says, smiling broader, "I'm gorgeous."

"You're alright looking." I shrug passing, careful not to trip over the new furniture to set my box down.

"As if." Amy scoffs, "Logan's a god among men."

Twisting, I give her a 'what the hell?!' expression while Logan chuckles.

"Look at this man," She says approaching him like Vanna White. Stepping behind him, he slightly raises his arms, glancing behind himself. Her arms come around his ribs, and my mouth drops open. What the hell is she doing?! Grabbing handfuls of his gray t-shirt, she pulls it up, "A god."

Logan's smile hitches on one side at the show she's putting on. I try so very hard not to look at his stomach, I really do, but it's damn near impossible to avoid. He's got tan skin stretched across a series of well-developed abs, not to mention one of those V things.

"A god." She repeats, smiling wickedly as she lets go and step back, "What about you, handsome?" She eyes Caleb.

"My wife hasn't complained yet." He says politely. My eyes immediately search his left hand, spotting the gold band I've never noticed before.

"Damn." Amy sighs, "Dee gets to have all the fun I guess."

Laughing, I raise my arms, "What fun? Logan's preparing me for Cole."

"Hard enough to forget Cole with any luck."

My eyes bulge at her innuendo, "We're not sleeping together."

"Probably should, I'd hate for you to go through life without knowing what an orgasm is."

"AMY!" I shriek, my body burns as a fine layer of sweat gathers in my palm.

"What? We're all friends here." She shrugs like she didn't just break about a million friend rules, "Hopefully some of us will get a little...friendlier."

THE ART OF DATING

I can't look at Caleb or Logan; I'm so embarrassed I could cry while strangling the life out of my former best friend.

"Where would you like us to move the couch?" Caleb asks after the silence becomes thick with my embarrassment.

"I don't care, against the window maybe." I point blindly across the room.

"You've always had it in here though." Amy pipes up.

I've about had my fill of her today, "Yeah well, shit changes."

"Jeez." She snides, dropping a box at my side, "Who peed in your oatmeal."

"You did." I whisper harshly, "What the hell was that?"

"Oh, chill out. It's not like they knew I was serious."

"Yes, they did! If you're so hard up for Logan, why don't you take him and leave me out of it, huh?"

"I don't want Logan; you guys are obviously hot for each other, I'm just giving you guys the nudge."

"I don't want to be nudged. He's helping me get Cole, that's it."

Knowing she's not going to see the wrong in the situation with a room full of people, I pull myself to my feet and busy myself in the bedroom until she comes in to apologize.

It takes the hardheaded asshole over an hour to do it, but eventually, I get the groveling I deserved.

"I'm wrecked." I sigh, flopping back on my new sofa later in the evening.

"At least we're pretty much done," Amy says from her spot on the floor.

"You guys want to order in? My treat." I offer, look at Logan and Amy in turn. Caleb ran off during my bedroom retreat earlier.

"Sure, what do you want Logan?" She looks up at him.

"I'm good for whatever."

"Italian or Thai?" I ask.

"Italian." They answer at the same time.

"You know, one day I'm going to replace you both with friends who like Thai food."

"Awe, we're friends, Duck?" Logan teases, sitting down next to me.

"When you're not an ass you are." I smile, pulling the online menu up.

"Why do you call her duck?"

"You already know why." I say with a warning in my tone. She promised earlier not to meddle and here she is, meddling.

"No, I know why you *think* he calls you that."

"And why does she think I call her Duck?"

"Cause I'm ugly," I respond to her, still scrolling through the app.

He laughs, his hand landing on my knee to give it a quick squeeze, "I made a joke, and the name stuck."

"What was the joke?" She inquires further.

"That I was turning her into a swan."

For reasons unknown my stomach does this little flutter, I shift in my seat to rid the sensation, "Okay," I say sitting forward, "Here's what they have."

We dined inside, choosing to watch a movie on my new smart tv until the night grows closer to dawn. Logan sits between Amy and I, with the exertion of cleaning and moving all day; I keep myself balled up in the corner of the couch to avoid another cuddle incident.

"I'm falling asleep," I say, climbing off the couch. "You guys can crash here if you want, I'm going to bed."

"Already?" Amy yawns, it appears she's trying to pretend like she didn't fall asleep against Logan's leg an hour ago.

"Yeah, it's almost four."

"Kay, I'll come with you." She says, stretching.

"You need anything?" I ask Logan who shakes his head, 'Okay, you know where everything is. If you leave just lock the handle."

He nods, his eyes holding mine for a moment too long, "Good night."

After another awkward moment of starring, he pulls himself together, "Night."

Slipping into my new bed, my mind tries to figure out what he was thinking when he zoned out on me. For a second I wonder if it was because I was taking Amy away from his lap when an unsettling feeling looms in my stomach, I try to shake it as fast as I can. I then lay awake in bed for an hour wondering why the hell that would bother me.

CHAPTER TWENTY-SIX

I feel rough when I wake up the next morning. We stayed up too late, and thoughts of weird feelings lead me to a very vivid dream about Logan, one that makes me blush thinking about it; don't worry the guilt of having such a dream while pining after Cole is enough to chase the thoughts away each time. Dunking my head under the stream of hot water, I try to forget about it, which is a little hard when it took place in this very stall.

"Logan here?" Amy asks, walking into my bathroom.

"I don't know."

"I have to pee," she says sitting down, "I left my phone out there last night, but I don't want to go out there looking like a hot mess."

I roll my eyes like that's even possible. She's photo ready twenty-four seven; I swear she's never had a bad hair day in her life, not even as much as an angry pimple in high school, nothing.

"You look fine," I tell her, yelping when the water turns to ice from her flushing.

She laughs angelically, leaving me curled against the wall, trying to avoid the spray.

Once the water is tolerable, I finish quickly, hopping out to dress in warm clothes and brush my teeth.

Wrapping a towel tightly around my hair, I follow the sounds of voices to my kitchen.

"What the hell is that?" Logan says by usual way of greeting.

"Clothing," I say, grabbing a bagel out of the blue box that I'm assuming Caleb dropped off. "What are you guys doing today?"

"I work at four," Amy says typing away on my laptop while Logan glares at me for talking with my mouth full, I give him a cheeky grin. "What about you Mr. Millionaire? Empires to build?"

"Nah, I did that last weekend, gets a little redundant after a while.'

I catch myself giggling and quickly stuff more bread into my mouth to stop it. What the

215

hell is wrong with me? If Logan weren't here, I'd be talking to Amy about my dream, but she's got a shit record at keeping secrets at the moment.

"You guys wanna go see a movie?"

Logan looks to me, telling me he won't answer until I do, "I don't know if you want to."

"Logan?"

"I'm fine with whatever you guys want to do."

"Good, movie it is. I'm going to get ready, so I can catch a cab to work afterward." She places the laptop on the counter next to me as she stands.

"I can have Caleb run you home if you need clothes."

"No need, I've got some here."

He turns to me for an explanation while my email loads, "One of those suitcases yesterday was hers. We leave clothes at each other's house for sleepovers-OH MY GOD!" I scream, jumping up, a shrill stream of excited pours from my mouth.

"What?" Amy and Logan both demand at the same time.

Ignoring them, I continue reading the email as my feet bounce up and down in a happy dance.

I scream again, looking at their confused faces then back to the screen. "Oh my god. Oh, my GOD."

"What?" Amy demands half annoyed, half already excited.

"I got an email." I shrug with a failed attempt at nonchalance. "Someone wants to hire me for their upcoming release."

"From who?" Amy asks walking slowly towards me, the smile she wears growing in size as her excitement escalates, even Logan moves around the counter in curiosity.

"Oh," I shrug again, an enormous grin plastered on my face, "Just Aimee Noalane."

The second her name leaves my lips, Amy screams just as loud as me, if not louder. Racing over, she links her arms in mine while we revert to our adolescence selves; jumping up and down.

In my moment of pure joy, I leap into Logan's chest, nearly tackling him to the ground. He wears a broad, yet slightly confused smile while he stabilizes my body.

"I'm very happy for you, but who's Aimee Noalane?"

My entire body goes as stiff as the pillars separating the two rooms, "You've never heard of Aimee fucking Noalane?"

217

He shakes his head, amused by my shock.

"She's only my favorite author of all time!" Pulling away from, what I now realize as a very inappropriate embrace, I rush over to my bookshelf pulling my beloved signed editions from their shrine and hand them to him, "She wrote the No Regrets series. I was so devastated that Damian was only a character that I actually cried when I was done."

"Is that like the main guy or something?" He asks, looking at each cover.

"Well, no. I have a thing for the bad boys in books, and he's totally swoon-worthy."

"Ugh, whatever, Oliver is way hotter." This is the only series I ever got Amy to sit down and read and the little traitor didn't even ship the same guy as me.

"Okay, well that's just not true, but I'll let it go, if I don't we'll get into another fight."

"You guys fought over fictional characters?" Logan's brow puckers incredulously.

"Yeah," She walks backward, out of breath from our freak out. "That's why I do my best to avoid books; I prefer the movies."

Logan hands me back the books that I gently place back in their rightful place, artfully draping the string of orchids across the spines.

"Aimee Noalane!" I squeal yet again.

Oh man, this just turned into the best day of my life.

Not going to lie, I have no idea what that movie was about, i was checking my phone every three minutes waiting for the email that included Aimee's manuscript. She's seriously the sweetest human being alive, and I just want to tie her up in my dungeon and make her feed me all the words. I'm declaring myself now; I will convince Aimee to write me a book about Damian one day, I'd be happy with a novella, shit even a short recap of his life events will do. It'll happen.

"So you know how you said we were friends?" Logan interrupts the silence while I fish around for my keys.

"Yeah?"

"I have an event next month, and I need a date. Would you be willing to do your old friend a favor and be my plus one?"

"Like a date-date?" It's a stupid question, of course, it's not a date. What's dumber is the fact butterflies are spinning around my stomach in anticipation of his answer anyway.

"No, not a date." He chuckles, deflating my stomach like a balloon.

"Oh, yeah, okay."

219

His lips curve to the right, "Can you come to my place Friday so we can go over what's to be expected?"

"I'm not going to see you until Friday?" I manage to keep the disappointment out of my tone. What is up with my emotions today? Maybe I forgot to take my birth control, and my hormones are screwing with my head.

He gently taps the top of my phone with his finger, "You're expecting something very exciting. I figured I'd give you the week off of boot camp to indulge."

A smile ghosts my lips, "Thank you."

"Don't mention it. I'll see you Friday, Duck."

Smiling, I push through my front door. He really is sweet when he wants to be.

Dropping my purse on the counter, I dig through it until I'm holding the little dispenser of pills, clicking open the dial I survey the dates. Sure enough, a little blue pill sits untouched. Breathing out a breath of relief, I pop it from its aluminum prison and swallow it.

For a minute there I thought I was developing feelings for Logan, good to know it was just a little hormonal imbalance. The pill is swallowed, and all will be right in the world tomorrow.

CHAPTER TWENTY-SEVEN

It's stupid how excited I am to be going over to Logan's. Not that my week break wasn't amazing, I've read Aimee's new book more times than I can count, devouring every line like a starving animal, my dungeon idea is becoming more of a life goal at this point.

Kicking the door, I wait, arms extending.

"Happy Friendiversary!" I cheer when the door swings open.

Logan, steps back with an amused grin, "Hey."

"I am tragically overdressed it seems," I say, taking note of his lack of clothing.

His chest is devastatingly bare, his muscles flexing with every moment, I blow out a breath while attempting not to gawk.

"No one's stopping you from walking around topless." He smirks, taking the cake from my hands.

"Well, it might be awkward for some people." A sing-song voice rings out behind him, and my stomach falls to my knees.

"Oh, my God!" I cover my mouth, "I'm so sorry! I should have told you the time I was coming over." I rush out, taking a step back, "I'm so sorry, text me when you want me to come back, or if you want me-"

"Duck." He says loudly, cutting off my ramble with a deep rumble of laughter, "Get in here."

"No, really, you're...busy." I wave to his bare chest, retreating further.

Stepping into the hall, he grabs my wrist, tugging me dangerously close to his bare skin.

"Joanna, this is Duck." That incredibly gorgeous blonde from Logan's Facebook steps forward, her kind eyes match her smile as she extends her hand to me. "Duck, this is my sister, Joanna."

"Oh!" I didn't mean to say that out loud, righting my features, I take her outstretched hand, "Hi, I'm Devina."

"It's nice to meet you."

"You too."

"So, what the hell is a friendiversary?" Logan asks, pulling out a knife as he inspects the blue frosting.

"We became friends four months ago," I shrug, trying to fight the blush against my skin, "It's a cheap excuse to eat cake."

"How come I didn't get a cake for the first three?"

"Well, cause that's what I'm calling your 'asshole faze'. You don't get cake when you're mean to me." I push him out of the way with my hip, taking the knife out of his hands.

Joanna laughs, "I'm going to go check on Stacey, I'll be back."

"Who's Stacey?" I ask the bitter little green goblin in my stomach rearing its ugly jealous head.

"The clothing designer," He says, stepping against my back, his hand comes around to adjust my hand, moving the knife, he pushes against my hand to cut a larger piece, "Jealous?"

223

THE ART OF DATING

I'm having trouble breathing. I think he's flirting with me, I mean, he's flush up against my back, his face dipped low, so his breath moves my hair with each word, he has to be flirting, right?

Swallowing hard, I shake my head like I don't notice, "Nope."

"Liar." His free hand pushes my hair over my shoulder, and my lungs stall, his breath grows warmer, the closer his lips get to my neck. Oh, fuck. He has to hear my galloping heart.

I need to stop him; this is wrong.

A small gasp steals my thoughts when his mouth presses into my neck. Oh, Christ.

"What are you doing?" I whisper when his lips leave my skin.

His hands twist my hips, putting us chest to chest.

"This." His hand threads in my hair while his eyes search mine, looking for any signs of protest, I'm ashamed to admit I don't have any. My face leans into his touch, his thumb gliding over my cheek. Oh my God, he's going to kiss me.

"Hey, Logan?"

Snapping out of my trance, I spin quickly in his arms, busying myself with cutting as Joanna reappears, "Whenever you guys are done she's ready."

"Okay. Hey, give us a sec?"

Her eyes travel over us suspiciously before nodding, turning on her heel she goes back the way she came.

"Hey,"

"Plates?" I ask as nothing happened.

"Devina,"

Braving my face, I turn to face him, "We can't."

"Can't what?"

Stepping into me once again, I fight with myself; my rational head against my traitorous body.

"This," I look down at our conjoined bodies, "This can't happen."

His fingers toy with my throat, "Why not?"

Swallowing, I release my bottom lip, "Because I think I might like it."

The corner of his mouth lifts while his eyes drop to my mouth, "That sounds like encouragement."

"It's wrong." I breathe, my chest heaves with every breath. "This isn't right."

His forehead creases while his thumb skims over my bottom lip, "Sure it is, it's just not right now."

225

Dropping his hand, he pulls away. My eyes fall closed as the breath I was holding slips from my lips.

"Stacey's waiting to dress you."

My mind is poisoned with thoughts of his closeness, my senses high off his cologne, his words don't have time to process, "What?"

"For the event next month."

"Oh," I nod, stepping away from the counter, "Yeah, okay."

Pulling away, I wipe my sweaty palms on my jeans.

What the actual fuck just happened?

LOGAN

After Devina pulled away for her fitting, I stood at the counter wondering what the hell was wrong with me. It's too soon, I know that, but when she got all flustered over Joanna and then jealous over the designer I was sure we were on the same page, and then I went and showed my hand too soon.

When she reemerged, she made it a point to avoid me at all costs, diving into a lengthy conversation with Joanna about books. It's amazing really, seeing her talk so passionately about something she loves. Four months ago it was like pulling teeth just to get her to admit she liked anything; now she's able to hold herself without any help at all.

I was able to keep her around for dinner and a movie, using her obsession with eating against her. Still, she only agreed after Joanna vowed to stay.

"I'm going to head out," Joanna whispers, standing up from the couch.

"Why are you whispering?" She nods to Devina.

Craning my neck; I see she's curled into a ball against the arm of the chair, fast asleep.

"I'll call you tomorrow," I tell her kissing her on the cheek.

"She's sweet."

"Duck?"

She laughs quietly, "That's a horrible nickname to give someone."

"I know."

"Then why do you call her that?"

"Because it drives her crazy."

"Is that the goal?" She chuckles, pulling the strap of her purse up her shoulder.

"No, but it's fun."

Giving me a bright smile, she shakes her head before turning for the front door.

Shutting the door behind her, I walk back over to Devina. Kneeling in front of her, I admire her button nose, the fullness of her bottom lip and the thick fan of lashes against her pink cheeks. She really is gorgeous.

Resting my wrist against the arm of the chair, I thread my fingers through her silky hair, "Hey, pretty girl."

CHAPTER TWENTY-EIGHT

"Hey, pretty girl." Logan's voice floats into my dreams followed by a touch so gentle it almost breaks my heart.

I don't want to wake up; this is too nice to give up. Here, I'm allowed to blur lines, venture into the unknown without any repercussions. A soft tickle dances across the seam of my lips, followed by a gentle pressure; this is so real, I feel the vibration of my moan as it leaves my throat. I love dreams like this.

My mind imagines it's Logan, his lips responsible. Working against the pressure, I kiss him back. Our mouths molding together perfectly; I wonder if my imagination does him justice. I'm not ashamed about pretending it's Logan; in the morning I can blame the movie and spicy food for my apparent fever dream, at this moment I just want to see how far I can go. As if sensing my thoughts, his lips force mine apart and another moan makes its way into his mouth.

Butterflies rip through my stomach, fluttering their way up my throat when his hand falls between my open legs. A light touch slides down the seam of my pants, circling back up with more pressure, making me gasp.

I feel his soft, dark hair under my fingers as they graze the back of his neck, the intensity of his fingers grows causing my back to arch into him, his hard body molding into my softness with the same perfection of his mouth. My hips rock against his hand, my nails grazing the skin of his neck.

With no obligations or expectations, I'm unashamedly selfish in my dream, taking what I want. Self-conscious thoughts cease to exist as I allow myself to fall over the edge. Sensation grips every muscle and nerve in my body at once, pulling them deep into my belly before releasing, waking every sense my body has to offer.

Crying out, I sit up, curled around something hard as wave after wave pushes through me from the tips of my toes to ends of my hair.

Holy shit.

Breathing heavy, I pull back as my body wakes up, small twitches pulse between my legs, I can't do that in real life, but I can have an orgasm in my sleep? Unfair doesn't even come close to how I feel about that.

Peeling my eyes open the world itself stops;

Logan.

Leaning above me.

Lips swollen.

His hand between my legs.

It wasn't a dream.

I stare at him in horror, watching as a slow smile grows.

"What just happened?" My voice comes out hoarse as I try to swallow the bile in my throat.

For the love of God, please tell me he thought I was having a nightmare, and his position is entirely coincidental.

His smile grows further, "I just watched one hell of a show."

"No," I start, not sure why that's the word that came out, I blame it on the fog surrounding my head while I desperately try to rationalize what just happened. "We didn't...?"

"We didn't what?" His smile fades as a mask of confusion takes hold of his features.

Looking down, my eyes follow his thumb that's idly rubbing my inner thigh, "Oh God, please no. We, you didn't, I didn't," I stumble over my words, my cheeks heat as my eyes begin to burn.

"Cum against my hand, fully dressed, in under three minutes? Sure did." His smile returns, pushing the hair away from my face. Cocking his head to the side, he observes me, "Why are you embarrassed?" His thumb brushes across my flaming cheek as I try to force back the tears.

Shaking my head, I pull away from him to stand on shaky legs. My eyes roam his apartment for my shoes and purse; I need to leave. Spotting both, I start forward just to be pulled back. My legs ache to run as fast as my pulse.

"Devina?"

"I need to go," I say, pulling out of his hold.

"Why?"

Shoving my feet into my worn boots, I collect my purse off the counter, "I just need to go."

Clasping both my arms, he twists me to face him, "What's happening?"

"I don't know." The first tear escapes and I try to hide my face, though he catches my chin forcing my eyes to his as he swipes it away.

"Why are you upset?"

My eyes fall on the couch while shame coats my skin and embarrassment pours from my eyes. His gaze follows mine before looking at me again, "Talk to me."

"That should never have happened; I didn't know it was happening."

A sad laugh causes me to look up, "How did you not know it was happening? You kissed me."

"I was sleeping."

He laughs again, "In what world?"

"This one." I sniff, trying to slow the tears that rain down. "I thought I was dreaming."

"You weren't acting like you were dreaming." His smile grows making me cry harder as a new wave of embarrassment sinks its claws into my stomach, his humor fades at the sob I try to mute, "Don't cry. Devina, that was hot."

"I need to go."

Stepping away from him, he steps forward, "Don't go, stay."

"I can't."

"It's after three, just stay the night."

I feel my head shake as I take another retreating step, "I'll get a cab."

"If you have to leave, at least let me take you." He turns to grab his keys.

"Please, don't. I'll be fine." Reaching blindly behind me I find the knob and twist, pulling the door open as he turns to look at me.

"I'm not letting you stand on the street this late."

"I'm sorry." Turning, I make my escape.

Pulling the door closed, I jog down the hallway to the elevator.

"Devina, wait." Pressing the call button repeatedly, I hear his footsteps close in behind me just as the doors open; he follows me inside, selecting the lobby floor.

"Please tell me why you're freaking out." He says softly.

I shake my head, unable to form words without letting the sobs break free.

One hand slips over my waist, turning me to face him as the other threads in my hair; his eyes search mine, "Don't be embarrassed. I wasn't lying when I said that was hot." He holds my face in place when I try to look away, "I've

235

never wanted anyone more than I did at that moment, watching you come undone like that...you're gorgeous." I bite my lip to the point of pain while his face falls in defeat, "I don't know what you're so worried about or what to say to make it better."

"We shouldn't have done that," I whisper.

"Why?" He asks his tone indignant. "Because of that fuckboy, Joel?"

"Cole." I correct automatically.

"Whatever, does he make you come alive like that?"

"That's not the point,"

"Then what is?" He asks, stepping into me, so I'm sandwiched between the wall and his chest, "Can he set your body on fire just by touching you as I can? How many orgasms have you had to fake because he was too selfish to get you off?" I push against his chest to no avail.

"Logan," I push harder against his chest until he steps back a fraction, it's still not enough to allow me the space I crave.

"Does he want to memorize the curves of your body or the sounds you make? Has he ever stripped away your clothes as well as your insecurities and just looked at you?" The elevator stops allowing cold air to rush in as the door opens. I try to pull free, but he smacks the panel, closing the doors, "Answer me."

Tears drip from my chin, unable to look him in the eyes, "No," I say softly, "He doesn't."

"I do." He says, threading his fingers through my hair once again. His mouths falls against mine, gentle but firm as his words resonate deep inside my chest.

There are too many thoughts and feelings rattling around inside me, none of them willing to stay long enough to dissect while his mouth works against mine, "Stay." He whispers against my lips.

Rolling my lips in, I give a weak push, and he steps back. Refusing to meet his gaze, I press the button to open the door.

I shove my body through before they're fully open and race across the lobby. Cold air assaults my face the moment I step outside, chilling the fresh tears, so they draw burning lines down my face as I run down the street. Thank God for New York; the city that never sleeps. I'm able to fall into the crowd, shielding me from Logan's searching eyes.

I make It twelve blocks before trying to hail a cab; eventually one spots me. Climbing into the back seat, I tell the cabbie my address and sit silently in the back, unable to keep myself together.

Pulling to the curb, I hand him my fare and climb out, disappearing into the building I rush to my apartment; collapsing into my bed in a heap of sobs and hiccups and I don't even know why.

CHAPTER TWENTY-NINE

I've avoided all things Logan for fifteen days, *fifteen days.*

He's called, texted, even buzzed my place a few times, but I've ignored it all. I still burn with embarrassment every time I think about what happened in his apartment.

I feel dirty and ashamed that I allowed him to do that while having the intentions of being with another man. It isn't fair to anyone; not to Logan, not to Cole, and it's not fair to me. Logan and I flirt, we play around with one another, but up until this point I always assumed it was innocent; then his candor in the elevator changed everything.

239

THE ART OF DATING

My head is such a mess of self-loathing I haven't even kept up my friendship with Ames. I throw her a lame excuse why I can't talk or come over and sink deeper into my head. I'm in love with Cole, I have been for five years, but Logan had a point; Cole never puts me first. I also believe I may have feelings for Logan now as well, which does absolutely nothing to assist in sorting out my emotions because I'm faced with the constant mantra of, I want to be with Cole, but I really want to kiss Logan again.

Dealing with all of this the last two weeks had left me emotionally and physically exhausted. So when my buzzer rang nonstop, I rolled off the couch in pure annoyance and slammed the intercom down, "What?!"

"Damn, with that attitude I should have brought forceps to remove the tampon out of your ass instead of this box of bagels." Amy's voice floats through the speaker.

"Sorry," I tell her, buzzing her in.

Walking over, I unlock the front door and reclaim my spot on the couch. After a few silent minutes pass a knock sounds against the wooden door, "It's open."

A brief pause, then the door pushes open. I see the blue box from Duffy's Bagels first, my mouth waters at the thought of food; I haven't had much of an appetite lately, but that box of buttery goodness can sway anyone.

As the box fully emerges through the threshold, I notice the hands holding it don't belong to Amy. Black boots come into view a millisecond before Logan appears.

"Hey." He says gently, standing at the threshold.

I lay there staring, he's got on one of those tight t-shirts under a brown leather jacket, and dark wash jeans; and it looks real good.

"Hi." I croak out, "What are you doing here?"

He looks over his shoulder then returns to my eyes, "You've been avoiding me, so I asked your friend for help."

"I'm not feeling well." It's not a lie, I may not be sick with a virus or deadly disease, but this event has my stomach rolling.

"Cramps?" The voice of my treacherous best friend trails into the room.

"No, traitor."

A blonde head pops through the door, peeking over Logan's shoulder, "Am not! I didn't know you didn't want to see him."

I raise an eyebrow at her, she tries to hide it, but I know her tell; her right dimple twitches whenever she lies, just like it's doing now.

"Okay, fine. I knew, but he wouldn't tell me why."

I wait for the twitch, but it never appears. Looking at Logan, I notice he's watching me; every shift, every tap, every breath I take his eyes document.

"What are you doing here, Logan?"

"Wanted to see you."

"Well, you saw me."

Amy's brow furrows as she looks at us, I hadn't noticed her enter the apartment or sit down beside the island.

"Oh, my God!" She gasps suddenly; Logan and I both turn to look at her. "You guys totally did it." An accusatory finger flies in my direction, "And you didn't tell me?!"

I roll my eyes, "We did not."

"We kissed, now it's weird," Logan says.

Amy's jaw drops, and I groan. I don't think this could be more awkward if we tried, I wish this couch would just suck all of my problems away, scratch that, I wish this couch would just suck me away.

"WHAT?!"

Instead of words, this odd noise comes out instead; Logan smirks at me while Amy continues to gape at us.

"Tell me everything!" She shouts. "Is he a good kisser?"

"Amy! He's right here!" I point to all six foot four of him.

"So?"

"We're not talking about this."

"Is it because he's a bad kisser?"

"Hey!" Logan complains.

"You're ripped, rich, and gorgeous. You can't win at everything, Logan."

The right side of his mouth tips up, "I don't know, Duck. Do I win at everything?"

"Shut up, Logan." I glare at both of them. "Leave the bagels on the way out."

"These?" He smiles, shaking the box, "Not a chance, these go where I go. I'm happy to share, but you have to talk to me first."

"We're already talking." I point out.

"Not what I mean and you know it."

I do, he wants to talk about that night and I really, really, really want to avoid it entirely. "I'm good; don't let the door hit you on the way out."

"You can't avoid me forever."

"I beg to differ."

"What happened?" Amy whines, "I need details, or I'm going to die."

"Don't you work today?" I turn my annoyance to her.

"Nope." She smiles cheerfully, "I get to watch this lovely soap opera unfold."

Logan's hand falls to his back pocket, producing a wallet. Carefully balancing the box of bagels on his forearm, he fishes something black out of the leather sleeve. "All expenses paid shopping spree for the next hour if you leave."

She pales at the credit card, "Are you serious?"

"She'll use up your entire line of credit in thirty minutes."

She glares at me while he holds the little rectangle of black plastic further in her direction, "Sky's the limit. Whatever you want, be gone an hour."

"Deal." She hops off the stool, snatching the card from his hand, "Later."

And just like that, I'm alone in my apartment with Logan.

"Bagel?"

"What are you doing here?"

"You're not picking up my calls, replying to my texts, or answering the door-"

"You'd think you'd pick up on the fact I didn't want to talk to you." I interrupt him.

"See, that doesn't work for me."

"So, to hell with what I want. Let's flash your money around to manipulate your way into my house uninvited and unwanted."

"Exactly."

"You're such an asshole. Ever think that's why I don't want to speak to you?"

"Nope, I think you don't want to talk to me because you're embarrassed about what happened."

"I don't want to talk about that."

"That's fine; I like listening to myself talk." I roll my eyes as he drops the box the bagels down on my cluttered coffee table. Picking up my legs, he sits down, dropping them on his lap. When I attempt to pull them away, he grabs my ankle, holding them there. "I think you're embarrassed, but I'm worried you feel I took advantage of you."

"I don't think that," I answer honestly.

"Well, that's good." He exhales loudly, "So it's because you're embarrassed?"

"I'm not embarrassed." I don't think.

"Then what did I make you feel?"

"Confused," I admit, pulling my bottom lip between my teeth.

He licks his, raising his eyes to mine, "You've got to stop doing that."

"What?"

"Biting your lip. I'm trying to do right by you and when you do that it becomes increasingly harder."

Is he admitting that I'm turning him on? "Habit, sorry."

"How did I confuse you?"

"Because you're not Cole," I answer honestly.

He laughs, "You're right about that, but go ahead and elaborate."

"I shouldn't be doing...things, with you, if I'm pining away for him."

He shrugs, "Why not?"

"Because I don't want to lose you when this is over. Lines are going to be blurred, and hearts are going to get broken."

He chuckles, "Who's heart? Are you admitting something there, Duck?"

Tugging hard, he finally releases my legs, allowing me to curl them tight against my body, "No, but I don't want to risk it."

"Are you scared you're going to fall in love with me?"

"You're so cocky. What if you fall for me?"

"I can fuck you without loving you."

Butterflies bounce off the walls of my stomach, "I'm the ugly duck, remember?"

Shaking his head, he stares at me before speaking, "You were never the ugly duck, just a little lost maybe."

Averting my eyes, I play with the sleeves of my shirt.

"I'm not sure what there's to be worried about, to be honest. Unless you're a virgin or something."

"I'm not a virgin."

"Then what is it?"

"I don't know, Logan! I've already told you that."

He scrubs his face, sighing. "What are you feeling?"

"Annoyed."

"I mean about what happened," He growls, "When you freaked out, what were you feeling?"

I shrug, "Embarrassment because I thought I was dreaming, ashamed, dirty, confused, and like a bad person."

"All that because I fingered you?"

"You did not finger me; my clothes were still on."

"Alright, all that because I *rubbed* you?"

"I don't know, Logan!"

"You do know," He says, leaning forward to dig into the box. Removing a bagel, he takes a

THE ART OF DATING

bite before continuing, "You just don't want to admit it."

"Admit what?" I've already confessed my emotions, what more does he want?

"You panicked because you liked it, you liked letting go, and the fact you were able to do it without Crull freaked you out."

"Cole."

"Whatever."

I sigh, adjusting so I sink deeper into the couch. I'm sure his reasoning is part of it, but it still doesn't feel like that's the whole story. Ugh, I hate being a woman; chock full of feelings and hormones that don't do anything but confuse you and get in the way.

"Admit it." He says, breaking the silence.

"That's not it."

"So, you didn't enjoy yourself?"

My cheeks burn as embarrassment rises to the surface, "Let it go, Logan."

"Look how red you're getting. Admit it; it'll make you feel better. I know it would make me feel better. I love knowing I'm the best at everything."

"I should lie just to bring your ego down a notch."

"So, you admit it then?"

"Fine! Yes, I admit I liked it. It freaked me out you could accomplish something in two minutes that he hasn't been able to do in five years, but that doesn't solve the riddle of why I want to puke every time I think about it or why I want to cry right now."

"Back up." His face lights up with that stupid smug smile, "What did I accomplish that he couldn't?"

A new wave of heat kisses my face, "Nothing, let it go."

"Sure will not."

"Why is this all on me?" I sit up to better face him, "What about all that stuff you said in the elevator?"

"What about it?" He asks around a mouthful.

"All that mushy, love note stuff."

He laughs, covering his mouth to prevent spitting bits of bagel across the room, "Telling you how badly I want to fuck you is hardly a love letter." Butterflies cannonball through my stomach.

"Not going to happen."

"Why not?" He asks, almost offended.

"Because you're helping me win back my ex? Don't you see how horrible of a person I would be if I did that?"

249

"You mean if you acted as though you were single?"

"No, it would be wrong to lead you on with the intent of being with someone else."

"I highly doubt you'd be interested in Noel after being with me."

"Cole." I correct, grabbing a bagel for myself. "And you and I are friends, right?"

"Uh huh."

"So, no sex." I shrug, the weight slowly starts to peel off my shoulders, maybe I just needed to talk to him all along.

"Why can't we be friends who sleep together?"

"Because that's wrong."

"In what world?" He laughs, "I'm single, you're single, I'm well aware of your plans to get back with Cal, you might as well get off while you can seeing as Big C isn't up for the job."

"Logan," I glare shaking my head, "It's not always about sex."

"That's where you're wrong. A relationship may not be built on sex, but it certainly depends on it."

"I disagree," I say, jutting out my chin. "I believe a relationship depends on the people involved. Sex is just a perk."

"You're not allowed to have an opinion until you've been properly fucked."

I glare at him, "I've had amazing sex, thank you very much."

"Tsk, tsk. It's not polite to lie."

"I don't lie."

"Then you clearly have no idea what amazing is."

"How would you know?" I huff.

"Because in five years he hasn't been able to get you off once, it took me, what? Three minutes? Imagine what I could do if I got you excited."

"I'd rather be loved than fucked; I don't need excitement."

The corner of his mouth rises in challenge right before my knees are grabbed and pulled towards him. My back hits the cushion with a thump before he crawls up my body. My food drops to the floor as his face nuzzles against my neck.

"Logan, get off me!" I try to push him, but the guy won't budge, "God, you weigh a ton!"

He chuckles, sending goose bumps to follow the path of his breath, "Do you feel the difference?"

"The difference in what, breathing and suffocating? If so, yes."

THE ART OF DATING

"You can feel excitement everywhere, can't you?" He tells me, his scent is an assault on my senses as it taints my oxygen, filling my lungs with all things him. His hand runs down my ribs as he speaks, "What would you prefer; this or scheduled coupling on Sunday nights after playing scrabble with Memaw?"

"My grandmother doesn't even live in New York, and I'm not that boring."

"Yeah, I call bullshit on that one."

"I'm not." I fight the tremble of my bones as my body comes alive beneath him. This is exciting, but I don't want it to be.

"Prove it then," His lips press against my jaw, running along my chin, "Kiss me."

"Friends don't do that."

"Yeah, yeah." He mumbles, threading his fingers through my hair, "We'll be friends in a minute."

His lips seal over mine as his hips grind against me, his fingers tangling further into my curls. I give in without wanting to, his lips demand and mine bow immediately. I fight the urge to grind against him, ignoring the ache to pull him closer and swallow every moan that attempts to escape as he shows me just what I've been missing out on.

Coming up for air, I glare at him, even though it's empty and try to wiggle out from underneath his body. "I hope it's out of your system now."

"Not entirely, but it'll do for now."

"Well, that's never happening again."

"We'll see."

"I'm serious," My glare becomes determined as we stare each other down.

Eventually, the fat lard moves off me enough that I can breathe without smelling his sporty scent.

"Fine, friends?" He says, offering me his hand.

I stare at it for a moment trying to find out if this is a trick or not. When I'm convinced he won't misbehave, I accept it, "Friends."

CHAPTER THIRTY

"This friend thing isn't going to work if you don't stop touching me all the time." I scold, removing his arm from my shoulder.

"No touching?"

"Nope."

"At all?" His face is scrunched in exaggerated disapproval.

"No."

"Not even a little?" He skims the pads of his fingers over the back of my hand.

"Stop," I warn, pulling my hand away.

"Why?"

Because I can't be trusted when you touch me? It's been nearly a week since we had our little talk. At this point, I think our lessons are just cheap excuses to feel me up. We've been practicing ballroom dancing for the event next week. Every day I'm forced to be pressed against his chest, and every day I have to fight the urge to give in.

"Cause friends don't touch like that."

"Maybe your friends don't, but mine do."

"Yeah, well you also sleep with said friends." I give him a knowing look.

"But not you."

"But not me."

"What if you change your mind?"

"About you touching me or my decision not to sleep with you?"

He laughs abruptly and shakes his head. "I was talking about me touching you, but now I'm intrigued."

"I'm not going to change my mind," I mumble, searching for the remote I just had. "About either of them."

"But what if you do?"

"Then I'll let you know."

He lets out a chuckle and hands me the remote that was wedged between the cushions.

"You'll tell me? When has a woman ever been so forthcoming about something she wants?"

"Why are you so chauvinistic?"

"Why are you so argumentative?"

255

"I'm not."

He laughs, "You're arguing right now."

"I'm arguing to prove a point."

"You're arguing to prove you're argumentative? I already knew that."

"Ugh, you're so annoying! No, I'm arguing because you're chauvinistic. Look, if I want you to touch me, I'll tell you. If I want to sleep with you, I'll tell you. I don't know why you keep throwing me into the lump sum of your prehistoric opinions of women but stop. I'm not like them."

"Believe me; I'm well aware."

"Then behave yourself." I elbow him teasingly and turn on the television.

"Just to be clear, I'm fine with both." He says standing up to stretch.

"Both of what?"

"Touching and sex."

"What?" I ask in genuine confusion.

"I'm fine if you touch me, and I'm always fine if you want to sleep with me."

"Oh, come off it!" I whine, throwing a handful of popcorn at him. "You heading out?" I ask, collecting the glasses and near empty bowl off the table.

"Are you kicking me out?"

"No, you can hang out if you want."

"Cool. What do you want to do?" He asks, slouching back onto the couch.

"I don't know."

"What would you be doing if I left?"

"I'm not sure, probably work."

"Work? It's almost midnight."

"I work better at night, it's weird." I start, loading our dishes into the dishwasher, "I have a hard time concentrating during the day."

"It's because you think of me, isn't it?"

"Oh, yeah. I just can't peel you from my thoughts." I answer sarcastically.

"I knew it." His head lulls towards me, smiling at me.

I roll my eyes in return coming over to sit back down.

"Alright, Mr. Excitement, what do you want to do?"

"It's Friday."

"Mhm."

"We have the entire weekend; I'm thinking somewhere warm and sunny."

I roll my eyes again and shake my head. "No."

"What? Why?"

"Because that's not normal."

"Who's to say what's normal? Why can't I take my friend to the beach for a weekend?"

"Because I don't want you to. It makes girls feel cheap."

"No, it doesn't." He argues, "Never, not once, have I made a girl feel cheap. I'm a surprisingly nice person."

"Well, that's debatable and anyway it makes me feel cheap. I'm not interested in your money."

He leans forward, so our faces are almost touching; his lips tug up on the side when my eyes fall to his lips. "I never said you were."

Looking away from him, I scoot back to gain a little room, "I've got a T.V if you want to watch something."

"You know, if you want to forget we're friends for a little while, I know something we could do."

"Stop it." I glare at him, though it holds no weight; the smile he wears tells me he's only kidding.

"It was just a suggestion."

"The answer's no."

"Suit yourself."

I can feel his eyes on me while I channel surf and it makes my body flush. I know what he wants, and I'd be a liar if I said I didn't want it just as bad.

CHAPTER THIRTY-ONE

"If Devina refuses to date you then I think we should make a pact." Amy smiles at Logan who leans against the bar next to her.

Apparently, she has world-changing news that required us to meet her at a bar before she'd tell us. She's been holding out on us for the last twenty minutes. Looking around the small establishment, I'm amazed by the drastic difference between the weekend crowds and this handful of Monday-night goers.

"And what's that?" He smiles.

"If neither of us is married in two years, we marry each other."

Logan laughs, looking at me. I give him a shrug, "We could be like siblings-in-law if that happened."

"Sure, Amy. If we're both still single in two years, I'll marry you."

With a proud smile, she raises her cocktail, "Deal."

Clinking glasses, they both seal their arrangement.

"Now that that's out of the way do your future wife a favor and give me a drum roll."

With a chuckle, he bounces his fingers off the bar counter.

"I have been named; wait for it...lead designer at Perkins fashion show this Friday." Squealing, she dances in place, linking her fingers through mine as we shriek at the top of our lungs.

"Congratulations!" I scream, more than half the bar is glaring at us, but I could care less because my best friend is going to be famous!

"I'm so excited!"

Letting me go, she hugs Logan. "You only have a week to prepare?" He asks, wrapping his arms around her waist in a friendly embrace.

I try not to be bothered by it, reminding myself it's Cole who I'm after, if anything I should be rooting for them, my two best friends marrying each other should be a dream come true.

"We have all of the clothing already," She pulls away, "I just have to create unique, and tasteful ensembles to highlight each piece for the spring collection."

"Congratulations."

"Thanks." Wearing a huge smile, she swoons against the bar. "It's Friday at nine, can you both come?"

"Duh!" I tease, she knows damn well I wouldn't miss this for the world.

"Logan?"

"I'd be honored."

"Okay." She claps her hands together, "Let's celebrate!"

Even though I was more than capable of taking a cab home from Amy's, Logan insisted on taking me home himself.

"What would be a good gift to get Amy?" He asks as we pull away from her apartment.

"For what?"

"Something celebratory."

"I don't know." I say, looking at the carpeted floor in thought, "I can ask if you want. Wait-" I hold my hand up as I think of the perfect gift. "It's expensive, but there's this red skirt suit that she's been going on non-stop about. I don't know how much it is or where to find it, but I can find out."

"Not now." He says when I remove my phone. "I want it to be a surprise."

"Okay, I'll text her tomorrow then."

"What do you say to going to dinner first?"

"She probably won't be able to because she has to get ready for the show."

"Okay, how about *we* go to dinner before?"

"Like a date?"

The right side of his mouth tilts, "Yes."

My stomach twists, I'm scared by the fact it doesn't feel like a negative twist, "Logan, I-I don't know about that."

"You've had dinner with me countless times."

"Yeah, but none of them were dates."

"Is there a difference?"

I scoff, "Yes, there's a difference. One is two friends getting dinner; the other is a date."

"Why can't it be two friends going on a date?"

"Because it's not right," I admit sadly as Caleb shoulders the car outside my apartment.

"It's four days away," He starts as I collect my purse from the foot well, "Think about it?"

263

"Sure," I promise.

He nods, "Until then."

My brow furrows, "Not tomorrow?"

He smiles, "Absence makes the heart grow fonder. Consider it my ploy to get you to say yes."

Giving him a small smile, I step outside of the car, "If I said yes, we both know we'd never make it to Amy's show."

Closing the door before he can respond, a giggle escapes me, "Night, Caleb."

Walking up the stairs my phone vibrates bringing a smile to my face. Fishing my phone out of my bag, butterflies take flight, but instead of flying up, they make a b-line towards my jeans.

LOGAN: If you continue to be a tease the next time I get you to say yes will be in quick succession while my face is buried between your thighs.

My eyes bulge at his text as my knees wobble.

Shovel, meet Devina. Devina, meet hole.

CHAPTER THIRTY-TWO

It turns out Amy wasn't due at the store until an hour before opening so filling Amy in on my plan; I texted a single word to Logan the next day; yes.

Dressing in a white button down top, I tuck it into my black skater skirt. Amy paired it with black stockings and a pair of red heels. She looks breathtaking in her red Chanel suit. She all but lost her mind when it was delivered to her door earlier today, claiming she was going to kiss Logan square on the lips when she saw him. He's unaware of my plus one to our date tonight.

I like Logan; I like him far more than I should so I don't feel the least bit guilty using Amy as my human shield.

The buzzer sounds in my apartment, informing us of Logan's arrival.

Amy giggles like a mad woman when I approach the intercom, "Shut up." I laugh, pressing the intercom, "I'll be right down."

"He's going to kill you." She laughs, handing me my keys.

"Yeah, but it'll be totally worth it."

High off the excitement of the evening, Amy and I act like fools on the ride down in the elevator; taking silly selfies and making snap stories in butchered British accents.

When the doors open, Amy runs full force into Logan, shoving her lips against his cheek, she gives him an obnoxious kiss, "Buy me things like this, and I'll marry you long before our pact."

"Congratulations on your event."

"Thanks. Are you surprised to see me?"

"I must admit that I am."

"Devina said you one-upped her and this was her getting even."

"Is that right?" His blue eyes land on mine, "And pray, tell, what was it that I did to deserve the pleasure of revenge?"

266

"You know," I smirk, rocking my phone back and forth in my hand.

"Are you teasing me?" He quirks a brow at me.

"Nope. Just getting dinner with my friends in celebration." I say passing him.

"I'm a man of my word, Duck." He calls after me.

"About what?" Amy asks, walking next to him.

"Nothing." I say at the same time Logan starts, "I told her if she insists on being a tease, the next time I'll-"

"Logan," I growl, shaking my head.

"What?" Amy whines, looking between us.

"Nothing. Let's go celebrate."

"That's not fair. You can't keep secrets on my special night."

"It's really nothing," I promise, holding the door.

Logan glares at me, pushing my hand away so he can take over.

"I don't think sex with me would be nothing." He smirks as Amy gasps.

"WHAT? You guys had sex?!"

"Shh!" I panic, flailing my arms at her while looking at Caleb who stands at the back door of the car, "No! We didn't do...that. He got pervy in a text, and I needed to shut him down."

"What did it say?" She says, ignoring my warning glances to shut up as we climb into the back seat.

"Nothing."

"Something." She puts her hands on her hip as Logan claims the front seat. "Logan, what did it say?"

Chuckling, he hands his phone to her, with him sitting in front of her, I wasn't able to intercept in time before her eyes read greedily over his text to me.

"Oh, my God." She chuckles, handing his device back to him. "Oh, my." Looking to me now, she laughs, shaking her head. "Why don't you guys just drop me and Caleb off somewhere, you can have the back seat."

"Amy!"

"What?" She laughs, and I think she's serious, "That's hot! If you don't take him up on that offer, I will."

Folding my lips in, I glare out the window. Well, this didn't go according to plan. I wanted to make this a non-date and have a little fun while I was at it, not be ganged up on. I'm not sleeping with Logan- I'm not.

The ride to the restaurant was filled with talk of Amy's show, much like our dinner conversation.

Finishing up our meal, Amy threw back not only the remains of her wine but mine as well. She claims not to be nervous, but her alcoholism suggests otherwise.

After being brought to our VIP seats next to the runway, Amy ran off for her pre-show prepping leaving me alone with Logan. Seeing as my blouse is form fitting and sized appropriately, I don't have any sleeves to twist, resorting to picking at the buttons on my cuff instead.

"Why are you nervous?" He asks after the eighth or ninth time my nail cracked against the plastic circle.

"It's nothing," I say, dropping my hands to my lap. "This is pretty cool right?"

He nods, still studying my profile. "Not that I don't enjoy Amy's company, but why did you bring her along tonight?"

Swallowing hard, I focus on the stagehand setting up a light stand as I speak, "Because I was scared to go alone. I don't want to mess up our friendship."

"Eating a meal with me would do that much damage?"

"If I agreed to go, on a proper date with you," My eyes find his, "What are the chances it would be more than dinner?"

His eyes drop to my mouth for a fleeting moment, "I don't know."

"If I gave you an opportunity to take it further, would you?"

"In a heartbeat." He answers quickly without a flicker of doubt.

"That's the problem. It can't go further."

"I think you're looking too far into things." He says leaning his forearms on his knees, "We've crossed that friend line on more than one occasion, and we're still us."

"And when Cole comes back?"

"You'll be back where you started," He smirks, "Boring and orgasm-less."

"Shut up." I push his shoulder, though it's half-hearted.

He's right; I was boring, and yes, orgasm-less as he worded it. Even though I don't see that changing, I know I can't sleep with Logan. My feelings for him are already much stronger than I care to admit, this would just complicate things, and I don't need that right now.

"You never lie, correct?"

I nod, off guard by his sudden question.

He looks away, nodding to himself. "Alright, then."

"What?"

"Nothing," He shakes his head, "I guess I was just hoping you wanted the chase. If that's how you want it, then I'll drop it."

He seems upset, not quite angry, more defeated. A sudden fear for our friendship threatens to choke me. "Are you upset with me?"

Pulling back, his brow furrows, "Of course not."

His fingers find the back of my neck, pulling gently into his shoulder he gives me a one-armed hug, kissing my hair.

"So what do we do now?" I ask, worried he's not being honest with me.

"We try not to blur any lines."

———

Amy's show is sensational. I sit proudly beside her as we watch her creations march up and down the little runway. Afterward, she's called up on stage where we all stand and applauded her efforts.

Happy tears sting my eyes as I watch her posing for the photographer with her models.

"I've never been so proud of her."

"It was a spectacular show, especially for only having four days notice. I've seen designers pull together a less impressive line with months of preparation."

"You should tell her that."

"I'm worried she'll float away, then we'll never get her back."

Laughing, I collect the program off the runway as she approaches.

Waving the little pink flyer, I return her bright smile, "I'm keeping this. It has your name on it."

"Want me to sign it?" She laughs, posing like nineteen-fifties actress.

I laugh, throwing my arm over her shoulder, "This was incredible."

"I know, right. God, I'm on cloud-nine." She swoons, leaning into my frame, "They're doing an after party down the street. You guys are more than welcome to come, but truth be told, I won't be available. Some suits are down and want to talk to me."

"Oh, my God! That's great!"

She squeals, standing up straight, "I know! I'm trying not to spas, but it's damn near impossible."

"Well, do you want us there? You know, for moral support?"

"Of course I want you there, I always want you guys around, but I'm going to be super busy, so I get it if you guys want to head home. I know you've got work to do."

"You sure?" Logan asks, pulling up to my side.

"Yeah," She waves him off, "I can bore you guys with all the details tomorrow."

"What do you say, Duck? After party or home?"

"Oh, don't give her that decision." Amy complains, smiling, "She'll come to support me, take her home. I'll call you tomorrow." She kisses my cheek before hugging Logan, "I've got to run, I'm catching a ride with my boss."

Watching her retreat, my heart swells at her success. Six years of climbing and she's finally making it to the top.

"It's only eleven," Logan starts, handing me my stuff, "Do you want to go home or see what the town's doing?"

"I should go home, try to get as much work done as I can before I'm woken up with the energizer bunny."

Logan growls, glaring at me, "That's the image you want to give me after telling me we can't move past friends?"

"What?" My face is so scrunched up, it hurts.

"You think I want to know that's how you wake up in the morning knowing I can't do anything?"

"What the hell are you talking about?" I ask my confusion transforming into annoyance. "You're not making any sense."

Pulling back slightly, he studies my face, "When you said you were going to be woken up with the energizer bunny what did you mean?"

"Amy. She's going to be bouncing off the walls with excitement. What did you think I meant?"

He chuckles, almost embarrassed, leaning on my shoulder he whispers, "I thought you were telling me you were going start your day with a vibrator."

Shooting away from him, the look of horror on my face is enough to make him laugh outright. "I don't even own one of those."

"That's a damn shame then, Duck. A damn shame."

CHAPTER THIRTY-THREE

"I feel like you're mad at me," I admit stepping out of the car in front of my apartment.

Logan hasn't spoken to me since the show, leaving a sheet of uncomfortable silence in the car on the drive over.

"I'm not angry."

"Then what are you?"

"Nothing." He smiles.

"I've never lied to you, the least you could do is offer me the same courtesy."

"I'm not lying, I promise."

"You haven't spoken to me since we left."

He laughs, "I'm sorry?"

"It's not funny, Logan," I whine, the pit in my stomach snarling with worry.

His laughter dies, righting his face, he looks me in the eye, "I promise. I'll see you tomorrow?"

That ugly feeling still sits in my bones but I try to ignore it, he said he promised. Nodding, I give him a weak smile, "Tomorrow."

"Sweet dreams, Duck."

"Bye."

Walking into my apartment, I throw my purse onto the counter with a huff. Why can't I rid the feeling that I've done something wrong? I can't be more than friends with him; it'll ruin everything. My feelings for him have already surpassed the friend zone; I know that I wouldn't be able to just sleep with him. He may be able to sleep with me without loving me, but I know that I'd fall for him if we did and I can't add that to my plate right now. It's better this way. I repeat that on a loop while kicking out of my shoes.

Just as I start to get the back loose on my earring, a knock sounds at my door. It must be Amy; she's the only one with a key who can get in.

Walking over, I unlock the deadbolt, cracking it open before continuing to work on my stuck earring.

"What happened, Ames?" I ask, pulling away.

"Devina?" Halting mid-step, I slowly turn to face the door.

"Cole?" I don't know why I ask that. I'm looking right at him after all. He's in a white tee, blue windbreaker, and jeans.

Oh crap, Logan never prepared me for this. What would he say? What would Logan say? *Men want what they can't have. Don't be a love-struck puppy. Be indifferent.* "What are you doing here? I'm running late."

"You look incredible, Dee." His compliment feels I don't know, wrong?

"Thanks," I say with a lack of interest, returning to the island, I grab one of my pumps and slide it back onto my sore feet. "Can I help you?"

"I just wanted to stop by and see if you wanted to talk."

"Can't." Grabbing the other shoe, I slide that one on as well, "Like I said, I'm late."

Grabbing my purse off the island, I step past him, closing the door behind me.

"I broke it off with Monica."

Thank God the key was already in the lock or else I would've dropped them and blown my whole nonchalant act.

278

"Sorry to hear it." Twisting, I give him an apologetic smile.

"I made a mistake; I want to work things out with you."

"Look, Cole. I don't have time for this." Pressing the call button, I twist to face him, "Logan and I are meeting Amy at the after party for her fashion show. If you want to talk, come by in the morning or something, but I can't do this right now."

"Oh, um, yeah. Great."

"Cool."

Stepping into the elevator, I immediately push the 'close-door' button even though I know he had plans on riding down with me. Rapidly pressing the ground floor, I count my blessings when it begins its descent, leaving him alone on the sixth floor.

Once the lobby comes into view, I duck into the community laundry room and pull out my phone.

ME: Cole just showed up at my door!

ME: I told him we were meeting Amy and I was late and couldn't talk right now.

ME: What do I do?!

ME: He's coming over in the morning to talk. We never got to I, N, or G.

ME: Ugh! Your silence is deafening, Logan! I'm hiding in my laundry facility awaiting your guidance!

LOGAN: Be there in five. Wait there.

ME: And if he sees me hiding in the laundry room?!

LOGAN: Go upstairs, if you cross paths tell him you forgot something. I'll be there soon.

Exhaling a deep breath, I push through the doors and rush to the elevator, I pray to my lucky star he's not on the other side when it opens.

Thankfully it's empty when I step in. I'm surprised by the flood of emotions currently going through my system. I wasn't *happy* that he came...I was terrified. But I don't think it was a good terrified; it feels more like I found my dad's porn stash, like I wasn't supposed to be there and now that he was, I feel almost guilty.

Explain that one.

CHAPTER THIRTY-FOUR

"Hey," Logan says, entering my apartment. "He leave?"

I stop pacing long enough to nod at him.

"You okay?"

"Yeah," I nod, but it's more to convince myself, "Why wouldn't I be?"

"I guess I was just expecting a different reaction."

"Like what?"

"I don't know excitement?" He chuckles.

"I'm just a little shocked I guess."

"Why?"

"Cause he just showed up, Logan! Without a word, he said he broke up with Monica and wants to try again. But, I wasn't happy when he said it, I felt like he wasn't supposed to be here. I was trying to get away from him, so I didn't

281

mess up, sure, but the other part of me just...had no interest."

The only sound to be heard in my apartment is the slapping of my bare feet on the tile as I continue pacing.

"Do you love him?"

Halting mid-step, I look at Logan who's leaning against my counter, his eyes studying me.

"What kind of ridiculous question is that?"

"An honest one."

"I've been with him for five years, Logan. I gave him my virginity, of course, I love him. You don't just stop loving someone who held that much of your life."

"But are you still in love with him?"

"I just told you that I was."

"No, what you told me was that he is a person that holds a piece of your life, Like Amy or Me, someone who inspired memories, someone you love. Being *in* love and loving someone are two totally separate things. When you're in love; that person consumes you. You go through your day wanting to make up reasons just to talk to them; you lay in bed at night eager to fall asleep so that you can play out all of your imaginary scenarios. There isn't a thing in this world or the next that would stop you from doing everything in your power to make them happy."

Staring at him while he speaks, I wonder who broke his heart. Who did he give everything up for just to be broken and thrown aside?

"So which one is he, Devina? Is he a *piece* of your life or is he your *entire* life?"

How the hell do you respond to that? Cole has been there from the beginning; he was my friend, my confidant, my happily ever after. So why can't I answer?

"It's not a difficult question."

"Yes, it is," I whisper.

"Why?"

"Because I don't know." I shout, throwing up my arms, "I don't know how I feel anymore. Six months ago I was ready to spend my life with him; I was ready to have his babies, I would have done anything to get him back."

"And now?"

"Now I don't know! He came by, and I was more worried about your reaction than his feelings. I was more concerned with getting out of here than hearing him out."

"So, let him go." He shrugs.

Scoffing, I turn away from him. "Let him go? Let the only person who's ever loved me go?

For what? Because I can't sort the chaos in the head? Because I let you kiss me? That isn't a reason to throw away a future."

"Throw away a future of what? Mistrust? Always wondering if you're good enough for someone who doesn't deserve you?"

"He made a *mistake*!"

"He *cheated*!" He yells back, rising up from the counter.

Since when does he feel like this? He's never voiced any of this before, "That was the point of all of this!" I cry, "To trick him into coming back!"

"The goal was to trick *you*!" He explodes, moving closer to me, "I had no intention of sending you back to that! I just made up all that bullshit, so I had a reason to be around you!"

"But all that stuff..." I trail off trying to make sense of this, "The clothes and how I looked and-"

"Was to build you up again! You had no self-esteem when I found you; you'd rather hide than be seen. I did that to make you see what the rest of the world sees when they look at you. That bastard snuffed out everything good in you and then tossed you aside."

"God," I mumble, pressing my hand against my forehead, "I don't understand any of this."

"Damnit, Devina!" He shouts in frustration. "What part of this is so confusing?" He takes an abrupt turn towards me.

Catching me off guard, I take a step back and bump into the wooden pillar separating the rooms. He closes the gap until we're almost touching.

"I'm in love with you." He breathes against me.

I need him to move away from me. I can't hold a coherent thought when he's this close, breathing the same air as me. His breath is a drug, and I'm a junkie desperate to get her fix.

"You can't, this isn't right, this whole thing is wrong."

He moves slightly forward, my skin catching on fire as our bodies touch. "Does this feel wrong?" He breathes, lowering his mouth to my ear, his hands slide around my waist. "Tell me I'm wrong."

I can't inhale, I can't exhale, and I'm scared to move. His breath dances across my neck and I'm screaming for my body not to bow into his. I'm trying to hold still, trying to remind myself not to give in, to protect myself. But the more his fingers dig into my flesh and the brush of his breath on my neck, the harder it is to think clearly. Every nerve ending in my body is a lit fuse, and every thought in my head is that of an addict. I want to give in; I want to give up.

"Tell me I'm wrong." His lips find my neck, and it's almost my undoing. "Say it, and I'll stop."

My hands find his; this is my last chance for distance; I can end this right now.

His teeth graze behind my ear causing me to inhale sharply; I feel his smile against my skin before doing it again. My body bends into him without permission, leading him on. But this is cruel; this is a cruel, sick game. I'm desperate to protect myself, but who's protecting him? I can't lead him on just to break his heart in the morning; I still don't know how I feel about Cole.

With all of my available effort, I try to put distance between us. Placing my hands on his chest I push, but he doesn't let go.

"Say it." He whispers, and it's a spell, a spell that threatens to pull me back into his alluring trance. But I can't be selfish, not with him.

"Stop," I whisper, barely audible.

His body turns to stone, but he doesn't pull away.

"Why?" He whispers without tone.

"Because- I can't think straight with you so close," I admit, slightly out of breath. This realization is somewhat embarrassing. What was I doing that would cause me to be out of breath?

"It's a simple question, Devina." He whispers moving his lips against my throat. "It does, or it doesn't."

"Please." I breathe the word at the contact.

"Please, what?"

He kisses my throat, and I want to scream and cry at the same time. I've never been so conflicted in my life. My body is screaming yes, but my heart is crying no. My fingers itch to touch him and my lips part to meet him, but my mind won't shut up long enough to let me give in.

"I can't." I give another feeble push to his chest.

His body remains against mine, but he pulls his head back to look at me. It hurts deep down inside to push him away when all I want to do is pull him in.

"You can't answer?" The corner of his mouth rises in a devastatingly attractive half smile.

I shake my head.

"I think you're scared." He brushes his nose along mine, and I die on the inside. I'm not sure how I'm still standing seeing as I can't feel my legs at this point.

"I'm not scared," I mumble.

"I believe that's the first lie you've ever told me." This contact is dangerous. "I know you feel it; so why are you pushing me away?"

"I'm trying to protect-" I inhale sharply when he trails his nose across my chin and kisses my jaw.

"Protect yourself?" He asks when I fail to finish my sentence; I can hear his smile.

"Not just me," He brings his face back up to mine and rests his gaze on me confused, so I continue, "If I'm protecting myself, then who's protecting you? I can't give in just to break your heart in the morning." I whisper, feeling the sting behind my eyes.

"That's what you're worried about?" He asks, almost relieved. It's not what I was expecting, at all. I nod. "Break it." He breathes with a smile, moving slightly closer causing my heart rate to spike. "It's yours."

He's painfully close. If I over pronounced a word, our lips would touch. "Just because it's mine to break doesn't mean I should," I whisper.

He closes his eyes and when they open they're darker, deeper. "Say yes."

THE ART OF DATING

My brow furrows in confusion, but his eyes give nothing away. "To what?"

His hands leave my waist and travel to my face, locking in my hair while his thumbs brush my cheekbones. Oh, God. With emotion caught in my throat threatening to give me away I gently shake my head.

"Then stop me." He whispers against my lips before closing the gap completely.

And. I. Break.

Everything breaks.

My knees,

My heart,

My will,

My self-restraint.

Though none of that seems to matter at this moment, I'm aware of it; I just don't care.

I'm kissing him back with the same fervor, the same passion, the same desperation as he's kissing me with and I'm lost.

Untangling his fingers, they fall to my waist, dipping under the fabric of my blouse to brush against my skin. His lips ignite the embers inside, his hands set my nerves on fire, his presence boils my blood.

Our mouths separate, precious air fills my lungs while he sucks and nips at my neck, traveling down my throat as deft fingers pop each button of my blouse, breaking contact briefly as the fabric is pushed off my shoulders, his mouth reconnects with my skin driving me further into the abyss.

He pulls me close to his body, one hand wrapped around my neck pulling my face back to his while the other steers my hips to grind against his. He guides me forward, never removing his mouth from mine until the couch is pressed against my calves. Gently steering me down, he lies me down onto the plush surface, his body covering mine while pants are undone. I'm about to tell him we need to stop this but the thought disappears when his hand slips under my skirt, rubbing against me.

Gasping, I arch forward into his chest. His teeth nip at my chin as an involuntary moan falls from my lips. Clutching his wrist, I hold on for dear life as his fingers do things to my body I didn't know were possible. All the while his mouth takes time memorizing every curve of my neck, the angle of my jaw, the contours of my lips, he takes his time; nothing rushed. Almost like every move is calculated, strategically planned over a span of fantasies. He's mapped out where and how to touch me to guarantee the most significant reaction.

Removing his hand, his fingers find the waistband of my skirt, slowly pulling, he robs me of my underwear, skirt, and stockings in one go.

"Up." He says, pressing a kiss against my thigh.

Crawling up to my knees, I watch him slide to the floor, his hands reach for mine, and I eagerly accept, allowing him to pull me forward. I don't know what he's doing and to be honest, I don't care.

"Put your knees on either side of my face."

My brow furrows, "What?"

"Just like I said."

Skeptically I obey, careful not to knee him in the face while I straddle his head. He wastes no time grabbing my hips and drawing them to his face as his tongue lays flat against me. Grabbing the back of the couch, I try not to grind my hips or buck against his face but its damn near impossible. My knuckles turn white against the strain; it's taking every ounce of willpower to stay upright when all I want to do is collapse into the sensation.

Pressure builds in my stomach, radiating in tingles across my skin as heat spreads down my thighs. I'm incoherent as gasps and moans leak from my lips; my forehead rests against my

291

wrists moments before skyrocketing backward. A strangled cry escapes my constricted lungs, my muscles painfully tight as a powerful wave of euphoria courses through my veins. It's too much; a sensory overload as my body gives into his demands, crashing my system into a twitching, writhing mess.

"That's one." He whispers, guiding my back against the cushions.

I've fallen so far down the rabbit hole, and I've left my rational thoughts topside. His face disappears between my legs once more; each exhale heats my exposed skin. His tongue draws a line up the center of my body until our mouths tangle once again.

Not possessing the acquired level of confidence needed for foreplay, I raise my hands to the hem of his shirt while he grinds against my pubic bone. He allows me to remove it, ebbing some of my embarrassment when I accomplish this with little to no error. Greedy fingers find his zipper as I attempt to free him, being horribly inexperienced; I make a mess in my efforts to portray sexy, growing more embarrassed the longer it takes to remove his jeans one-handed. Thankfully, Logan's hand falls to the opposite hip and assists, his clothing melting away leaving only flesh on flesh as his body sinks against mine.

He's rock solid underneath smooth skin. My fingers explore the craters of his stomach while his lips follow my clavicle, his hand running between the couch and my back, gently lifting me, his mouth travels down the valley of my chest while deft fingers unclasp my bra, the material slides off my shoulders, exposing my chest. He assists its journey to the floor while our mouths clash together in a passion only fit for movies.

I'm pulled onto his lap, my knees falling on either side of his hips while his hand disappears between my legs. I feel him sliding himself up and down, a shudder shakes my body at the sensation, moaning as he slowly lowers me on to him, his hips making small bobbing motions as I stretch around him. I feel my nails dig into his shoulders, but they're unresponsive to my orders to stop.

Needing more; I gently rock my hips, bringing a groan to rumble in his throat, his hands digging into my ass, his thumbs pressing against my hips as he guides me. The pressure of his invasion transforms to blissful friction as my body accepts the fullness, allowing him to start moving.

Every time he spears his hips forward, he pushes me down, both clawing at one another, groaning and moaning together.

Shifting his weight, I'm laid down, my hands caught between gripping his arms and clutching his shoulders while his hips continue to push me closer to that building pressure.

"Logan," I whine, my knees molding against his hips, my head pressing deeper into the cushion, my body tightening in preparation to explode. "Logan."

"I know, baby." He growls, "Just let go."

My lungs burn, my knuckles are stiff, and then I ignite. My scalp prickles, goosebumps race neck to toes as I scream out.

An animalistic growl shakes my bones while his hand tightens painfully around my hip, he mumbles some sort of profanity, lifting me to bury himself as deep as he can possibly go before stilling. Groaning, I feel him pulse inside me as my limbs continue to twitch on their own accord.

"That's two." His voice husky as his shoulders rise and fall to the same rhythm as mine.

I'm exhausted, my body hums but burns at the same time, my throat aches, and my eyes are heavy.

"I think that's enough for now." Lifting my chin, he kisses me long and slow, draining me of the last shreds of energy before drifting off to sleep.

CHAPTER THIRTY-FIVE

An annoying rap against my front door stirs me awake. My naked back is pressed against Logan's front, my head on his outstretched arm. I don't know when we eventually transferred to my bedroom, but this has to be the best night's sleep of my life.

His fingers tighten around my hip when I try to climb out of bed, "Just stay."

"Someone's going to knock my door down," I rasp, "It's probably Ames, I'll be right back."

He lets go to roll on his back, the arm I used as a pillow drapes over his eye while the other rubs his chest. My lips curve on their own accord as I lean into the bathroom. Pulling my robe from its hook, I quickly cover myself, tying the sash just as I reach the front door.

"Hey." Cole's standing in front of me, his eyes looking me over in mild confusion,

"What's up?" I ask, smoothing my bed head.

"You told me to come by this morning."

Oh crap! I totally forgot about that. "Oh, yeah."

His face falls further as he takes in my less than enthusiastic tone.

"Tell Amy if she didn't bring bagels she's not allowed in," Logan calls behind me.

My face scrunches together as my eyes fall shut. Well, this isn't awkward.

Forcing my eyes open, I hold up a finger, "One minute."

Closing the door, a laugh bubbles to the surface, "It's not Amy!" I stage whisper, Logan's standing in my kitchen, loading the coffee pot wearing only his briefs. "It's Cole!"

The muscles in his back tense before he turns around to face me, "What does he want?"

"Last night I told him to come back, remember? He said he wanted to talk."

He nods, his face void of any emotion, "What are you going to do?"

"I don't know," I whisper back, glancing at the door like it might confirm that we're not being overheard. "That's what you're here for; you're supposed to be my guru or whatever."

I watch his fingers tap on the edge of the counter while his eyes focus on the tile, "So you're still going through with it? Getting him back?" His eyes rise to mine, disappointment, and pain lingering in their depths.

"I don't know. Things have kind of changed here don't you think?"

"So tell him to fuck off." He shrugs.

"I can't do that," I whine, checking the door once again, I'm taking too long in here.

"Why do you keep looking at the door?"

"Because he's out there!" I whisper-shout at him.

"So? Tell him to get lost."

"Logan." I pin him with a glare, "I told him to come back, I can't just tell him to leave."

"Why not?"

"Because," I don't have a reason, it just feels wrong, "I don't know, okay. Just tell me what I'm supposed to do because my ex-boyfriend is standing on the other side of this door waiting to come inside where the guy I just slept with is half naked in my kitchen."

"Who do you want?"

"What?"

"Who. Do. You. Want?" He says slowly, pulling away from the counter, "Him or me? Because you can't have both."

For crying out loud, it's been less than twenty-four hours since we hooked up and I haven't had my coffee let alone time to process what happened or how I feel about it. "I don't exactly think now is the time to discuss this."

"I think it's the perfect time." He stops in front of me, his fingers picking up a lock of my hair before letting it fall between his fingers. "Who is it?"

My mouth gapes like a fish, too many thoughts and not enough seconds to work through them.

"When you think about a day from now, maybe a week or next year, who do you see?" His eyes search mine as I think about my answer. The truth is, I don't know who I see. I see Logan in everything, but there in the background lingers Cole.

Logan's fingers slide against my throat, slowly rising to capture my jaw, "I don't know."

"Yes, you do." His eyes bore into mine, "You're either scared of saying it isn't me or you're afraid to give up the safe alternative outside that door."

"Logan," My eyes glance at the door once again, causing his hands to fall. "He's waiting."

He laughs without humor, his eyes looking up, tracing the lines of the ceiling. Pulling away, he walks towards the bedroom.

"Logan," I call after him, he neither stops nor turns around.

Closing my eyes, I take a deep breath, opening the door once again, "Hey, sorry. It's just gonna be a few more minutes."

He inhales likes he's going to speak, but he's not my priority right now. Half jogging, I run after Logan, finding him dressed, sliding his keys and phone into his pockets, "Don't be mad."

"I'm not mad."

"Then what are you?"

"I don't know, Devina." He says, facing me. "I really don't."

He scoffs when all I do is stand here and stare at him, his eyes look around my bedroom, pausing at the bed longer than anything else, "Does he love you?"

His question catches me off guard, my words tumbling out in response, "I don't know, yeah? Why are you asking that?"

"Do I love you?"

A nice little fissure starts at the base of my heart, last night he said he did. "Yes."

His lip curls as he shakes his head, "And you still don't know who to choose?" His features turn angry as he marches towards me, "You didn't have to think about my answer, you already knew. You questioned his. Here's another one for you, does he love everything about you? The way you chew on your lip when you're nervous, or the way you ramble on about books or find it endearing the way you light up when you see food? Or what about this, does he make you a better person or does he shut you down until you seek refuge in oversized clothing, hiding behind glasses and messy hair. Because what I see in front of me is a far cry from what I met five months ago."

I search for words, for answers to his questions; I try to get anything out of my mouth while my eyes sting with unshed tears.

"He *cheated*, Devina. How can you still want that piece of shit?"

Pressing my hand against my forehead, I beg anyone who will listen to press pause on my life, to give me a few minutes to deal and understand. I hear everything he's saying, I do, but I've gotten myself into a serious hole right now, and I'm panicking.

"And all this means nothing." He sighs, hurt and frustration roll off him in waves.

"It means everything," I whisper, cause it does. It holds a weight I've never felt before.

"Apparently not because your still not seeing it."

It's like he's talking in code, "Seeing what?"

"That I'm the better man! That I'll never do to you what he did! That there isn't a single thing about you that I'm not completely and utterly in love with."

"It's only been five months." I voice out loud; it's not enough time to feel that way about someone.

He pulls back slightly, "Do you love me?"

I feel my eyes expand at his question; I'm not ready to answer that, my mouth once again opens and closes as I search for the answer.

"If I walk out that door right now and never come back, how would you feel?"

Devastated, abandoned, like a piece of me would go with him. But, I also feel that way about Amy. How do I find the lines when I'm still trying to comprehend everything at once?

He laughs without humor, "Nice."

"Logan," I try, but he raises his hand to silence me.

"It's cool. You got him back, just like you wanted."

Pushing past me, I try to catch his arm, but it slips through my fingers, "Please, don't leave." I rush after him, "I don't know how I feel. Everything's happening so fast, and I can't keep up. Don't take my silence as an answer just because it's what you want to hear."

Spinning around so quickly I nearly run into his chest, as he holds the knob of the door, 'What I want to hear? You think I want to hear that you love that worthless piece of shit more than me? You think I want to hear silence after telling you I'm in love with you?"

"That's not what I meant; I'm just asking you not to take my silence as an answer to anything. It's easier for you to get mad than understand I have things I need to think through."

"That's the problem," He says in an eerily steady tone, "There isn't anything to think about; I love you, he doesn't. I raised you up; he tore you down. I give, he takes. But it's fine, Devina, you need time? Take it, but don't blame anyone but yourself when the harsh reality of what's behind that door slaps you in the face and I'm no longer here."

"I'm not choosing anyone right now; I just need to sort everything out."

"Good thing there isn't a choice to make any more."

His words chill through the fabric of my robe; frost blooms in intricate designs against my skin, while my chest gets encased in ice.

"What do you mean by that?" My words come out hoarse and low as fear chokes me.

With the twist of the knob, he yanks it open, his eyes hold mine, engraving his anger and pain onto my soul as he talks to Cole, "She's all yours. Might want to let her shower me off first."

It's like I've been shot in the chest, my breath is knocked from my lungs in a jolt of pain. Tearing his eyes away from me, he pushes through the stairwell door.

Silent tears slip down my cheeks as I stare after him, not even the echoing thud of the heavy metal door closing is enough to pull my gaze away.

"Hey, you okay?" Cole asks, his hands feel foreign and unwelcome as they slide up and down my arms.

Shrugging myself free of his hands, I retreat inside. I make it to the corner of the kitchen counter before my body halts from the excruciating pain surging through my veins, poisoning my body with every beat of my heart.

"Hey?" He tilts my face up, and I pull it out of his hands, "Dee." He laughs grabbing my chin again. "You did the right thing."

"What the hell are you talking about?"

"Dumping that loser." He nods to the door and then smirks.

"I didn't dump him," I groan, trying to free my face but he holds tight. "Let go, Cole."

"I just got you back, Dee." He says with a smile I no longer long to see, "I just want to," His eyes drop to my lips before I have a chance to stop it, he seals his mouth over mine.

It's wet and uninvited; it's a strange realization to find my body rejecting him just as hard as my affections.

Pulling away, I grab his hands and pull hard, "How does Logan taste?"

He stops fighting me, releasing my face immediately. "Ew, Devina, what the hell?"

His face curls in disgust as he steps away from me. I have absolutely no remorse to offer. "Do you want to order us some food or something?" He plops down on my couch like a potato. When I don't answer, he stops fumbling with the remote long enough to look up at me. "What?"

"Why are you here?" I ask, not recognizing my own voice.

"You told me to come by."

"After you showed up unannounced. What did you want?"

"Well," His shoulders drawing back, "I wanted to talk to you, about us."

"What us?" I laugh without humor.

Sensing my lack of interest, he sets the remote down and slowly stands as if I'm a wounded animal. "There's always been an us, Dee."

"Was there an us when you were fucking Monica Claire?"

My use of the word 'fuck' makes his eyes bulge, "I don't know what you're asking."

"Was. There. An. Us. While you were bent over that whore in our bed? Or when you moved her into my apartment? Was there an us when you decided to cheat on me?"

"Hey, Dee. Look, that's the other reason I wanted to talk to you. I made a mistake, a foolish, selfish, unforgivable mistake." I nod along in agreement. "And for that, I am so sorry."

We both go silent; he stares at me while I stare at the wall behind him. "I think it stopped being a mistake the moment you made the decision to do it," I say with a sudden air of clarity.

"Wha- what are you saying?"

"I'm saying it stopped being a mistake when you chose her over me." My eyes fall to his, "Not only did you go through with it, but you continued to do so. How long were you cheating on me before I caught you?"

His eyes plead with me, "Please don't ask that."

"How long?"

He takes a deep breath and blows it out through his nose, "After her second novel."

I gasp, blinking hard to make sure I'm awake, "That was three years ago."

He nods, "I don't know why it happened or why it continued...it just did."

"Why didn't you tell me? Or break up with me? What was the point of keeping me around?"

He shrugs, "I knew you wouldn't leave."

"Excuse me?" I ask in genuine shock, "I did leave."

"No you didn't, not really. You kept us as your profile picture for months; you never told anyone we broke up and you didn't ask me to leave until you started seeing that rich guy. I knew this," He points to air between us, "Was going to happen. You love me, Devina. I knew that if I just got it out of my system you'd take me back, at that point, I could give you myself completely."

"So because I loved you that was permission to treat me that way?"

"Don't act like the only victim here, okay. I messed up but so did you."

I pull back, appalled, "How?"

"You let yourself go; you climbed into your stupid little books, stopped going out. You changed."

"When have you ever known me to be anyone other than who I am? I never liked going out, that was always what you wanted, and I stopped caring about my appearance because you'd get angry if anyone looked my way because to you, I was dressing up to impress other people, that I was fishing for compliments from other guys.

Jesus, I've been blind this whole time. It's like the blindfold has been lifted as everything falls into place. It was never my choice to stop doing these things; it was done to avoid an argument. I altered myself to fit him, a triangle peg trying to fit into a square hole. We were never more than a show, a grand game of pretend. God, I'm such an idiot.

I realize he's yelling about something when I interrupt, "It's time for you to go."

Stepping to the threshold, I pull the door open, meeting his eyes.

"What the hell happened to you these last couple of months? I don't even know who you are anymore."

"That's because you never did."

"What?"

I smile at the ground, a true genuine smile.

"What are you smiling at?"

"I just realized something that took entirely too long to see." My smile grows as my heart warms my chest, waking the butterflies in my stomach, "You need to leave."

"And what'd you realize?" His body posed in challenge.

"That I'm in love with Logan." I smile at him.

His face turns a nasty shade of red, the veins in his neck raising with the increased blood flow, "You whore."

"I hope you find peace, Cole. And love, and happiness, and all that other stuff, I really do. But you're a square hole, and I just don't fit."

"What'd you call me?"

"It's time for you to leave."

"Fuck that! I'm not leaving."

"Kay, well lock up when you leave then."

Still, in my bare feet and robe, I shut the door, running for the stairwell. Taking two steps at a time, I race down the flights, convinced my feet will get me to Logan faster than the elevator. I just hope Caleb is still caught up in morning traffic; he never had time to call him and arrange to be picked up.

Breaking through the lobby floor my heart beats painfully in my chest as my lungs scream for oxygen, ignoring the burn of my muscles, I race through, completely unfazed by the looks around me until I'm outside. My head swivels up and down the street, desperate to find him. Please don't be too late.

There. I see a shiny black car, the back door open as someone steps inside.

"Logan!" I yell with everything I have, pushing past the congested sidewalk.

The closer I get the more I can see him, one leg steps inside, the other holding his body upright, as his head swivels in my direction. "Logan!"

His eyes find mine, an incredulous smile playing on his lips. His hand bounces off the roof of the car while he shakes his head and then

climbs

into

the

back.

"Wait!" I cry, pushing harder to get through, "Logan!"

It's not too late; it can't be. Finding no mercy in the crowd, I shove my way to the street just in time to see them pull away.

CHAPTER THIRTY-SIX

When I got back to my apartment, Cole was gone.

Grabbing my phone I tried Logan about a thousand times, each unanswered call more painful than the last. Still, I dragged clothes over my body, locked up the apartment and hailed a cab.

I feel like I'm running on autopilot as I hand the cabbie my fare and climb out in front of Logan's building.

Realizing I don't have an access key, I mask my features and approach the desk.

"Hi." I smile cheerfully, "I forgot my keycard for the elevator."

"Name?"

"Devina Anderson," I say, looking over the counter trying to get a peek at her screen. With mild annoyance, she twists the screen away. "I come in almost every day to see Logan Devitt."

"I know who you are." She replies in a bored tone. "You aren't listed as an authorized user."

"I know. I was using his driver card before."

Picking up the receiver her red painted nails punch in a four number code, "Mr. Devitt. This is Charlene at the front desk. There is a Miss Devina Anderson here for you, sir. She says she misplaced her access key, shall I make her another?" Her eyes shoot to mine while she listens to whatever he's saying before darting away, "I understand, sir. Enjoy the rest of your day. Uh huh, you too. Bye-Bye."

Hanging up the receiver she avoids eye contact, "Mr. Devitt isn't expecting any appointments today."

"That's bullshit." I snap, drawing her stricken gaze to mine, "Call him again, let me talk to him."

"Absolutely not." She puffs her chest, "Now I suggest you leave before I have you escorted out."

I growl, pulling at my hair as I look around. Someone has to rent out the other apartment on his floor; maybe if I hang out on the elevator long enough, someone's bound to go up there right? Except there are four elevators, they could take any of them leaving me with a twenty-five percent chance they'll choose mine.

Just as I start to turn away, I hear the same loud thud that rings in my apartment day and night. Twisting, I catch sight of the stairs through a small rectangular window. I don't need any more thought, in the event of an emergency they aren't going to make someone scan a card to get to the stairs.

Hope blooms in my stomach, he'll have to open the door eventually.

"Miss Anderson." The clerk calls in a clipped tone, "Miss Anderson."

Pulling the door open, I glance over my shoulder long enough to see her raise the phone to her ear, her eyes pinned on mine. I cock a smile and race forward.

On the second floor, I jumped into the hall and called an elevator in the event she was calling security. Selecting the little seventeen, I pray for a miracle, the scan device blinks red. Damn. Moving down each floor, I wait until one lights up.

The fourteen lights up allowing me to breathe a sigh of relief at only being three floors

314

below him. I bounce from one foot to the other as I impatiently wait for it stop. Thankfully, no one in suits and earpieces jumps out at me when the doors pull away to the fourteenth floor. Nervously glancing over my shoulder, I jog across the hall to the stair access door.

My legs burn, but I push forward until I see a large seventeen painted in thick black letters against the brick wall. I can't help the smile that engulfs my face, making this last flight the easiest. It fades just as quick when I tug on the door to no avail. The sound of metal slamming into metal echoes around me. It's locked. The fucking emergency door is locked.

Frustration wraps a noose around my neck, cutting off my rational thought. I pull, I push, I kick, pound and beat on the door while tears of frustration blur my vision.

Logan's apartment is on the side of the hall so he probably can't even hear me beating the crap out of myself against the door.

My arms sting and my legs ache as my body slowly slides down to the door. I will him to come outside, to sense my presence.

Pulling my phone out of my pocket, red, stiff, fingers unlock the device, calling his phone once again.

THE ART OF DATING

Approaching footsteps from the flight below sends my heart racing. Closing my eyes, I feel the tears fall as I will him to answer. I just need a second, one tiny, insignificant second in this world of time.

"Seventeenth-floor stairwell." A man speaks at my feet, "I found her."

"I just need to talk to him." I sob, still pressing the phone against my ear.

"You need to leave, Miss."

"I just need one second. Please." I open my eyes, begging him to make the exception, "Please, just get him out here."

He doesn't reply as he reaches down, taking my arm into his hands and lifting me to my feet.

"Please, I made a mistake." I cry, "I should have told him I loved him this morning, but I just didn't see it. Please, help me."

"Down we go." He says, steering me down the stairs. Looking over my shoulder, I beg the world to make him appear, but he never shows.

Mr. Security Guard uses an access key on the sixteenth floor, allowing us to use the elevator to the ground floor where I'm walked out like some hobo who drinks too much. But that's not enough; he holds onto my arm until a cab pulls to the curb. Opening the door, he continues to hold me until I'm fully seated.

I give my address to the cabbie through hiccupped sobs while the man shuts my door.

Giving up on trying to call him, I open my messages,

ME: It's you, it's always been you. I was just too blind to see it.

CHAPTER THIRTY-SEVEN

Today...

So you can see what I'm talking about when I say that one action broke two hearts. One stupid, insignificant moment of silence destroyed everything; I destroyed everything.

Logan won't answer his phone; he won't text back. I can't get to his apartment, especially since I was escorted out yesterday, and I don't know where Caleb parks the car or what he does when he's not playing chauffeur. I'm all out of options, and I've never felt as helpless as I do in this moment.

What's wrong with me? How could I have not seen this? Logan was there from the start, he never once tried to change me or force me to be someone I wasn't; he gave me the tools needed for me to find myself. How was I able to stand in front of him and not see the fact that I love him? How was it possible to be so naive? So spoiled and ignorant? Logan poured his heart out to me and what did I do? I threw it back in his face so I could give some nobody the time of day? Logan was right; there was never an option. it's him; it's Logan, Cole never stood a chance.

Sucking in a sharp breath, I wrap my arms tighter around my chest, trying to hold myself together because if I let go, I'm going to splinter into a thousand pieces.

I love him.

I love him more than I've ever loved anyone in my life.

I love him; then I broke him.

I'm more upset about breaking his heart than I am about his silence.

I deserve this pain; he gave me his heart, and I threw it away. I may not have cheated, but I'm no better than Cole; I took Logan's love for granted, convinced it would be there when I wanted it and gave my attention to someone else. Cole doesn't deserve a second chance so why the hell would I?

Suffocating on the thoughts, I pull my phone to my face, dialing through the tears and hold it to my face.

Two rings later, a chipper greeting rings out through the speaker. I sniff hard, trying to find words. "Devina, what's wrong?" Amy's concerned tone makes it difficult to inhale.

"I need you." I manage to choke out.

"I'm on my way." I nod, even though she can't see me before hanging up.

Dropping the phone to the mattress, I give into the sobs that break my ribs, rock my chest, and rob the air from my lungs.

CHAPTER THIRTY-EIGHT

Amy let herself into the apartment; it didn't take long for her to find me curled against the mattress. Without a word, she crawled up beside me, pulling me into her arms. I cried harder as her arms tightened around my shoulders, understanding I wasn't in a place for words, she simply hugged me until I eventually cried myself out.

Sniffing hard, I attempt to swallow the hiccups that pop painfully in my chest.

"What happened?" She says gently, her arms still tight around my shoulders.

"I ruined everything."

"With what?"

"Logan," my voice cracks as a fresh wave of tears surface, "I'm in love with him."

"I know." She coos into my hair.

"You do?"

"Of course I do," She chuckles sympathetically, "Sometimes I think I know you better than you know yourself."

"Why didn't you tell me?"

"You needed to figure it out for yourself."

"I fucked up, Ames."

"How? What happened?"

"I slept with him."

"Logan?" I nod against her shoulder, "When?"

"Night before last."

"What's so bad about that?"

"He told me he loved me."

"But that's a good thing." She chuckles.

I shake my head remembering the hurt and anger on his face, I should have known right there that I was making a mistake, "But Cole showed up."

"Oh, no."

I nod, "Logan told me to choose, and I was so confused with everything that was happening that I couldn't. So then he asked me if I loved him and I told him I didn't know." Another hiccup forces its way out of my chest,

322

while tears rain down, staining my pillow with their salted sorrow, "But I do. I was talking to Cole, and it just hit me. I told him to leave, and I chased after Logan, but when I got there, he took one look at me and left. He didn't even let me talk to him, so I caught a cab to his place where the stupid bitch at the front desk called security and had me removed, he told her not to let me up."

"He had you removed?" Her tone protective.

I shake my head, "No, he told her not to let me up so instead of leaving I ran up the stairs hoping I could get in through the emergency doors but they were locked. I tried calling and texting him, but he won't respond. He won't even read my messages; both text and Facebook are unread. He hates me."

"He doesn't hate you." She says quickly, "Maybe he's just busy."

I scoff, wiping my nose on the back of my hand, "No, he's not. He doesn't want to talk me. God and why should he? I broke his heart."

"Devina." She sighs, "You both have a right to feel hurt and angry, but it's not like you did it intentionally. He's known where you stood with Cole this entire time and it's not fair that he would blow up on you for being confused."

323

"He told me he loved me and instead of giving him a chance, I threw it away to hear Cole out. Who, by the way, has been sleeping with Monica for three years. That's what I gave Logan up for."

"But I thought you said you couldn't choose?"

"I couldn't, at least not right then anyway."

"Well, if you didn't choose, then how did you give up Logan?"

"I let him leave when I should have run after him. I knew he was hurt and angry and I still let him walk out the door."

"He'll get over it," She coos, running her fingers through my hair, "He's going to see the missed calls and messages, and he's going to realize you picked him."

"I'm too late, Ames. You weren't here to see the look on his face when he left, or hear how he made me sound like a one night stand."

"That's just the anger talking, you know that's not how he feels."

"I don't know, Ames. If he didn't mean it, why hasn't he responded?"

"Because he's probably just as upset as you are, put yourself in his shoes."

"He's never going to talk to me again then." I interrupt, gagging on my tears.

"Yes, he will."

"I wouldn't talk to me."

"Yes, you would." Her stern words cut through the humming in my head, "Give yourself some credit, Dee. He's hurt, and he's angry, he needs time to cool off. You'll see."

"This happened yesterday morning; he can't at least read the messages?"

"He's probably busy." I shake my head, knowing he's not. It's Sunday, he doesn't do anything on Sunday's, and we all know it. "Here, you want me to call him?"

Yes. "No."

"Yes, you do. Here, hop up."

Sitting up, my head feels like it's full of wet cement, my nose is clogged, and my throat feels raw.

Amy pulls her phone out of her jeans pocket and unlocks it while scrolling through my contacts. Once she finds his number, she transfers it to her phone and selects the speaker icon.

My heart hammers in my chest as I watch the seconds tick by. I've wished he'd answer just one call this entire time, but here I am, staring at her phone, praying he doesn't.

"Hello?" My heart slams into my stomach so hard; I fear it might fall right through the mattress.

"Hey, it's me," Amy says casually while staring at me, making sure I manage to keep myself together.

"What's up, Amy?"

"Have you talked to Devina today? She hasn't texted me back so I thought she might be with you."

There's a long pause while we both stare at the phone, "I haven't talked to her since yesterday, try Cole."

I suck in a breath to tell him I sent Cole packing when Amy pins me with a glare that promises immediate death if I blow her lie.

"Why the hell would I do that?"

He laughs cold and bitter, "Look, I know she's there with you, you wouldn't have been able to get my number any other way. I refuse to compete with that asshole; I'm not going to be a part of some high school love triangle. I told her where I stood; I said my peace, now I'm done."

"Okay, but don't you think you should talk to her-"

"No, hence the silence. I've always liked you, but this isn't your fight. She made her choice, and now I've made mine. I'll see you around, Ames."

The line dies, and I think I do too.

What the fuck have I done?

CHAPTER THIRTY-NINE

"Babe, come on." Amy shakes me from my current resting place. Over the last five days, she's been taking care of me. And by taking care I mean she holds a mirror under my nose to make sure I'm still breathing. "I have to go back to work tonight, and I need to know you're up and about."

"I'm fine, Amy."

"No, you're not."

Sniffing, I try to hold the tears back, "You're right, I'm not."

"Get up, or I'm calling Logan."

Just hearing his name hurts like hell, "He won't answer. Trust me; I've tried."

"Girl, don't test me. You know I'll do it just to prove you wrong. Do you want him to know you haven't showered in five days?"

"Like he'd care."

"Okay, well, I do. You reek."

"I do not."

"You're used to the smell. Come on, before you get bed sores." She pushes me closer to the edge of the mattress until I almost topple over.

"Just shower, okay? I don't need you to pretend like you're not hurting, I don't need you to go out and join the world, I just want you to stop smelling like death."

"Fine, but I'm coming back to bed."

"Fine." She surrenders her hands.

Slipping off the mattress, I haul myself into the shower.

Opening the door to let the steam escape, I pause, toothbrush in hand when I hear Amy crying. Throwing my toothbrush down, I run down the hall to see her on the sofa, phone in hand.

"What's going on, are you okay?"

She silences me with a wave of her hand.

"It's an emergency; there's been an accident, I need to talk to Logan." She pauses to listen to the line before continuing. "I don't know if she'll make it that long."

What the hell is she doing?!

I watch as real tears form in her eyes as she coughs out another sob. "Okay."

Wiping her nose on her sleeve she looks up at me, "She put me on hold." She says in a clear, unfazed tone, "He's been out of town I guess, isn't supposed to be home until tomorrow, I think she's tracking him down."

"What the hell are you doing?!"

"Getting Logan to talk to you."

"How?"

"I told the woman at his apartment there was an accident."

"Amy!"

She ignores me, putting her phone down on the coffee table before selecting the speaker icon, a waiting jingle sings through the speakers while I sit down beside her.

"Hello?"

"Yes, I'm here." Amy cries, it's like a switch; one minute she's Amy, the next she's a grieving mess. Maybe we should have moved to L A to pursue acting careers instead.

"His sister is listed as his emergency contact."

"That's Joanna," I whisper.

"Joanna, yeah."

"I can relay the message if you'd like. She might be able to track Mr. Devitt down."

"Please, yes. I don't want her learning of the accident this way, please inform her it's an emergency, and she needs to call me back immediately."

My brow furrows, what the hell is she doing? Amy gives the receptionist her phone number before hanging up.

Wiping her eyes, she smiles at me, "Pretty good, right?"

"What are you doing having Joanna call you? The plan was to get him to answer, not freak out! When he finds out I wasn't hurt he's going to be even angrier!"

"I'm not telling her you were in an accident. I'm calling her for back up."

"Back up for what? That's his sister; she's team, Logan."

"You don't know that."

"Yes, I do! They're close, Ames. If you didn't want to talk to someone and they called me, I'd tell them to go fuck themselves."

"Not if you knew I was making a big fat mistake."

"It's not going to work."

331

"Oh, stop being such a Debbie Downer, let's just see what she says."

"If she calls."

"She will. It's an emergency remember?"

Rolling my eyes, I sink further into the couch, this is going to end badly; I know it.

"She's calling!" Amy shrieks, running out of my bedroom with the phone held out like it's on fire.

"So, answer it!"

"What do I say?"

"You don't know what to say!? This was your idea!"

"Shit, I know! Hold on. Hello?"

My body goes cold as my heart skips a beat, "What is she saying?"

Amy shakes her hand at me in a silent gesture to shut up, "Yeah, that was me. Okay, so, please don't hang up. My name is Amy, I'm friends with Logan," She nods, "Yeah, well I'm also best friends with Devina...Yeah, okay well have you heard the latest gossip on them?...Okay, well Logan told Dee that he loved her, then they slept together, then her ex-boyfriend showed up...hold on, hear me out.

She kind of freaked out and didn't know what to do, see she has this problem with having to please everyone and you see she didn't want to be a jerk, well Logan got mad and left. Devina told her ex to go fuck himself and went after him, but he's ghosting her. I love your brother and all, but he's being a total ass about this and won't even hear her out...yeah she's here." I shake my head while slashing my throat, "'Kay, here she is."

Handing the phone out, I glare at her, "Some best friend you are."

"Shut up and talk to her."

Groaning a sigh, I raise the phone to my ear, "Joanna?"

"Hey, so what's going on?"

Rolling my eyes, I flop back onto the couch, "I don't know. Amy had this idea to tell his apartment that it was an emergency to get him on the phone. She's the mastermind behind all of this."

"But like, what's going on with you and Logan?"

"Nothing. He won't talk to me."

"That doesn't sound like him. What did you do that pissed him off so bad?"

"He told me he loved me, and I didn't say it back, I didn't know what to say, I was so overwhelmed that I just stood there like an idiot and he stormed out."

"So, he's avoiding you because you broke his heart and your best friend thought it was wise to call me and what? Confess?"

"I don't know why she called you."

Ripping the phone from my hands, Amy puts it on speaker, "I called you because I need you to get Logan to talk to her."

"Whoa, this isn't my fight. Logan's a big boy; he can make his own decisions. If she isn't in love with him, I'm not going to help her hurt him more. Let them work it out themselves."

"Clearly you don't get it. Dee loves him; she just didn't know it at the time, everything was just sort of dumped on her at once, and she needed a beat, one your brother wasn't willing to give."

"As I said, this isn't my fight."

"Well, I just made it your fight. The apartment said he'd been gone? Where is he?"

"Why are you the mouthpiece here? If Devina wants to talk to him, then she needs to do it by herself."

"She did, and he had security remove her."

"He did not." I groan, "The woman at the desk did."

"Am I on speaker?"

334

"Yep."

"Why am I even involved? Are we not all adults here?" Joanna groans.

"You're involved because we need your help."

Joanna sighs into the phone, "He'll be home tomorrow before his flight, talk to him then. That's all I'm willing to say."

Without a further response, she hangs up.

"That went well," I tell her, tears stinging my eyes. I knew this was a crapshoot from the beginning, yet, here I am feeling the last ray of hope leave my system.

LOGAN

"Hey." Joanna saddles up beside me, taking the mess from my hands, unwrapping the felt tie, she refolds the tissue paper.

"Thank God you're back. I think I ruined most of your supplies," I laugh looking at the disaster before me; mutilated paper and ties lay in heaps across the table.

"I should have known better than to put you in charge of this." She smiles, "You heading home before your flight tomorrow?"

"No, I'm going to spend the night at a hotel tonight. No point in driving home just to come back up."

"What about Devina? Are you sending her home with Caleb?"

My heart drops at her name, "She's not coming. Riding solo tonight."

"What's wrong? Was she busy or something?"

I pause longer than I want to. "Yeah, something like that."

More like busy moving her ex back into her place. In what fucking world does he deserve any part of her? How, in all of this, did I get it so wrong? From day one it was always about him, she made that point perfectly clear. So, naturally, I'd offered her my heart knowing damn well she wanted someone else's. Good, smart move on my behalf.

"You guys have a fight?"

Turning in my seat, I eye her suspiciously, "Why would you ask that?"

Shrugging, she keeps her eyes on her task, "Something about the tone of your voice. You've been sulking since you drove up here and now she's not coming."

"I have not been sulking, I've been busy helping you prepare for this event, which we're still behind on. Guests will be arriving in less than half an hour."

"You forget I've known you your whole life; you can't pretend with me. I know when you lie and I know when you're hurting."

"Let it go, Jo," I tell her, standing. I have no interest in talking about Devina. She's already on my mind twenty-four-fucking-seven; I don't need to relive it.

"Did you fall for her?"

Stopping mid-stride, I face her once again, "Why would you ask that?"

"You look miserable, she's not coming, and you're lying about why she's not here," She shrugs, "Two plus two equals four."

Running my tongue over my teeth, the hole in my chest smarts. I love the girl, but she doesn't love me back, if Jo had her heart rung through the ringer as I did, I'm sure she'd look miserable too.

"Drop it. I'm going to check with the stage manager and make sure everything's set up. You need to start getting ready."

"Logan."

Turning one more time, I face her with a sigh, "What?"

"Talk to her; you may not know all the facts."

If it wasn't for the fact Jo doesn't have a Facebook and that she and Devina never exchanged phone numbers, I'd think they were communicating. "You know something I don't?"

"Just that..." Running her hand through her hair, she sighs, twisting on the stool to better face me, "If you wait too long, you might lose her forever."

"I already have."

CHAPTER FORTY

Lying in bed, I watch the minutes tick by on my laptop as the saddest songs YouTube has to offer play through the speakers when my phone goes off in quick succession. Pulling my still vibrating phone off the bedside table, I scan over Amy's messages;

CROTCHSNIFFER: FWD: I, in no way, condone this kind of behavior from adults. With that being said, if my brother's going to act like a child, then I see no reason to feel guilty treating him as such. This is where she can find him.

CROTCHSNIFFER: FWD: [ATTACHED ADDRESS]

CROTCHSNIFFER: FWD: His plans have changed, he's no longer returning home before his flight. I've sent Caleb to collect her. The event has already started, if she leaves immediately, she might be able to catch him before he goes.

CROTCHSNIFFER: GET YOUR ASS READY-NOW!

CROTCHSNIFFER: NOW!

CROTCHSNIFFER: YOUR LACK OF REPLY BETTER BE BECAUSE YOU'RE GETTING READY!

ME: What the hell am I supposed to do? Show up, unannounced and force him to talk to me?

CROTCH SNiFFER: YES! That's exactly what you do! Find his sister; she'll help. GO!

Oh man, what the hell am I doing? Climbing out of bed, I hear the buzzer go off. Running through my apartment, I press the intercom, "Yes?"

"I've been sent to collect you."

"Fuck, that was fast. Alright, I'm coming." Granting him access into the building, I run back to my bedroom, hearing him tell me he's sending the elevator up through the speaker.

Looking down, I cringe at my blue sweater and spandex shorts. Oh well. Scooping my boots off the floor, I rummage through my drawer for a pair of socks. Grabbing the first thing I see, I

341

rush back out grabbing my keys off the counter as I pass.

This is by far the stupidest thing I've ever done. Padding down the hall, I enter the elevator in my bare feet.

ME: Jesus! How long ago did she text you? Caleb's already here!

CROTCHSNIFFER: I was with a customer, I sent them the second I read them. Are you going?

ME: I'm in the elevator.

CROTCHSNIFFER: OMG! THIS IS SO ROMANTIC!! It's like the perfect ending to your very own romance movie!

ME: IF he talks to me.

Shoving my foot into the first sock on, I groan. I grabbed a pair of black thigh highs from last year's Halloween costume. This is already turning out to be a disaster.

The elevator opens, just as I'm pulling the zipper up on my boot.

"Miss Devina." Caleb nods, walking in front of me to open the door.

"What the hell am I doing, Caleb?"

"You can figure that out in the car, this way."

We walk down the street, finding the black car parked crooked against the sidewalk. Car horns sound as they have to pull into the other lane to pass it.

"Don't worry about my door," I tell him, grabbing the handle. "I got it."

He goes without argument, both of us falling into the vehicle.

What the fuck am I doing?

CHAPTER FORTY-ONE

We made the hour and a half drive in forty-five minutes thanks to Caleb's speeding. Thanks to his knowledge of the event, I know that everyone will be outside, his family's table is near the stage.

I still have no idea what the hell I'm going to do or what I'm going to say. I don't know if he'll give me the time of day, even having Joanna in my corner doesn't help my nerves. It's not her who I'm trying to convince.

"Good Luck."

"Thanks, Caleb."

Walking up the cloth walkway, I find myself horrified. Everyone is seated under extravagant white tents, dressed in tuxedos and ball gowns. This was the event we were supposed to be attending together, the night I met Joanna, I was fitted for one of these gowns, and here I am looking like a cheap hooker.

"I can't do this," I tell Caleb, rushing back to the car. "I look like a prostitute someone left in their limo. I can't go out there like this."

"You aren't one of those women," He nods in the direction of the event, "That's what Mr. Devitt liked the most about you. You are unashamedly yourself. Don't be afraid to shine, remember the sun doesn't care if it blinds you."

"Did you just make that up?" I asked, shocked by his little pep talk.

He shakes his head, with a smile, "My wife posted that on her Instagram this morning, it seemed fitting. Now, be brave."

"What if he won't talk to me?"

"He will."

"But what if he doesn't? Then I'll end up embarrassing myself in front of all those people. I mean, have you seen how many people are here? There's like a thousand of them."

"And not one of them knows who you are. I can take you home, or you can do what you came here to do."

"If your wife messed up, like really, really, really messed up and you thought she didn't love you back, what would you do if she showed up here?"

"I would expect a grand gesture, something to prove she was worth my time."

"Like what?"

"I couldn't tell you; you'll know what to do."

I read books, I've lived vicariously through thousands of lives, surely I can think of something.

I nod my head, "I can figure it out."

Nervously approaching the party, I'm stopped by a man in a tuxedo at a podium, "This is a closed event, ma'am."

"I'm a guest."

He eyes me incredulously, making his disappointment in my attire well know. "Name?"

"Devina Anderson, I'm attending with Logan Devitt."

His gaze shoots to mine in shock before he rights himself. Searching a list his pen stops abruptly, leaning forward, I catch sight of my name.

"Do you have I.D?"

"Oh," Crap. "No, I didn't know I needed any. Mr. Devitt's driver brought me; he can verify who I am if you need."

"Were you informed this was a black tie event?"

"Joanna has my gown." I feel my cheeks pink with the lie.

"Be sure to change immediately."

"Thank you." Slipping past him, I keep to the dimly lit areas, my eyes searching for a familiar face.

Making it all the way to the stage stairs, I still haven't caught sight of Logan or Joanna. Pulling out my phone, I send a quick text to Amy,

ME: I can't find Logan or Joanna.

CROTCHSNIFFER: Where are you?

ME: Next to the stage.

CROTCHSNIFFER: So get on the stage.

ME: Not funny! I'm freaking out! I'm dressed like a slob and sticking out like a sore thumb.

CROTCHSNIFFER: I'm serious, Dee. Get up on the stage, he'll see you.

ME: And run in the opposite direction from embarrassment.

CROTCHSNIFFER: Stop being a pussy. You're whining and chickening out. Get your ass on that stage and give him one hell of an apology. We've all seen the end of this movie. You make this epic speech about how you love him, and he'll sweep you off your feet.

ME: This isn't a movie.

CROTCHSNIFFER: OMG. JUST. DO. IT. It'll work.

The next text is a GIF of Shia Labeouf.

I can do this.

I'm determined to do this; *I can do this.*

My feet fall on each step as I slowly climb up to the stage. He poured his heart out to me; I can do the same, *I can do it, I can do it.*

My ratty combat boots sink into the carpeted surface as if I weigh three times my weight. Lights blind me with their heated rays as I reach the podium.

The wood is warm under my hands, a speaker aimed at my face. *I can do this.* My gaze lifts and I watch as thousands of people start to notice me. *I can do this.* Just like in the movies, *it'll work, I can do this.*

Raising to my full height, I look over the crowd hoping to meet his eyes, the lights beaming down on me throw a sheet of white haze making it hard to tell one face apart from another. No matter, I got this.

Leaning forward, I clear my throat into the microphone. *This will work. This will be epic.*

"Logan Devitt." My voice rings out across the event, loud, clear, and oh, God, what have I done.

Everyone's staring at me in my oversized sweater, thigh highs, and raggedy boots while they're dressed like royalty in floor-length gowns and tuxedos.

The knot in my chest grows too heavy, falling to my stomach with a weighted splash causing bile to rise in my throat and panic to race through my veins. *I don't got this*, not even a little bit.

"Um...your, uh, your car's about to be towed." I cringe at my pathetic attempt at a love speech, pulling away from the podium.

Just as I turn to quickly to run off the stage, I hear his smoky voice crack through the speakers surrounding me.

"What the hell are you wearing?"

I laugh, forcing myself not to cry. Blinking the tears back, I shield my eyes from the glare of the overhead light, trying to find him in the crowd, "I left my 'Fuck the Haters' hoodie at home, I had to improvise."

"What are you doing here?"

"Where are you?" Silence falls as I look around, everyone sits staring at me. Through the thousands of faces I see, none belong to the one person I want to see the most, "Logan?" '

"To my understanding, this was a black-tie event; even Bill Cosby hung up the sweaters once in a while."

"This wasn't exactly-"

"You're going to need to talk into the microphone if you want to be heard." His voice interrupts.

My knees shake with nervous energy as I bring my face closer to the microphone, all while my eyes search for him, "I was saying this visit wasn't exactly planned."

"No kidding. Is there a reason you decided to crash my parent's anniversary event?"

I cringe, "I'm very sorry, Mr. and Mrs. Devitt. I, uh, need to talk to your son."

Oh, this isn't like the movies at all. I can't recall a single one where the heroine puked all over the stage from embarrassment.

"So talk."

"I think it would be more respectful to your parents if we took this somewhere not so…" Dramatic? Awkward? Humiliating? "Public."

"I don't know about the crowd, but I'm quite enjoying this little show."

A few chuckles interrupt the silence; it takes everything I have not to call them suck-ups. My heart is going to pound right out of my ears, and they're all laughing.

"Please, can we like, not do this here?"

"What was your plan, Devina? You had to have some sort of intention when you marched up here, and I know it has nothing to do with my car. So, what is it?"

"I wanted to get your attention."

"That's it?"

Gnawing on my lip, I glance at the crowd hoping they'd lose interest. No such luck, we have everyone's undivided attention. "I wanted to talk to you."

"So talk, but make it quick. I'm sure your boyfriend will be expecting your return, and we have a party to resume."

"You know, you're a real asshole sometimes. If you would have picked up your phone, just once, you would have known I told Cole to leave minutes after you walked out."

"If that's all you have to say, I'll get someone to call you a cab."

Throwing my hands out in defeat, the tears I promised to swallow start to pour from my eyes, "You know what? If anyone should be up here apologizing, it's you. You dumped everything on me at once and didn't even give me a chance to talk. If you had just waited, you would have heard me tell him that I was in love with you. It's you, Logan, it's always been you, and I'm sorry that I didn't see that before. You don't have to love me back, but you can't remove yourself completely from my life. It's hard enough to lose your best friend, but losing the person you love at the same time is sure to kill me."

Movement catches my eyes, through the screen of unshed tears I see him emerge from the shadows of the stage. He's in a tuxedo looking every bit as beautiful as when he's lounging in a pair of jeans or making coffee in his boxers.

"I'm stupid, and I'm selfish." I tell him, "I know I don't deserve anything from you, but I'm asking for it anyway because I love you, Logan."

I hiccup, watching him come towards me. I can't slow the stream of heartbreak as it cascades in rivers down my cheeks. Closing my eyes, I beg for this to be real, there's a high probability that I've passed out from embarrassment, and this is all a hallucination.

The all too familiar sporty scent invades my senses as my face is lifted, I don't have time to open my eyes before his lips crash into mine. His mouth is greedy, taking everything I came here to say and so much more.

My fingers clasp around his wrist, keeping him close while his thumbs brush the tears away. His lips molding against mine, he's my triangle hole, and I fit perfectly.

"That was single-handedly the most awkward display of love I've ever seen." He says pulling away, the corner of his mouth rising into a devastatingly sexy half smile, "But damn it all if it wasn't the best thing I've ever heard."

I smile through the tears that his thumbs continue to brush away. Squeezing his wrists tighter, I sniff back my emotion, "I love you, please don't walk away again."

"Sweetheart," He smiles sadly, "I'll never walk away from you again."

"Promise?"

"Yeah, Duck. I promise."

EPILOGUE:

"If any of you kiss my girl on the mouth, you'll be shitting out teeth for the next week."

"Oh come off it." Joanna scolds at the same time Amy says, "You said that last year."

I smile, watching him draw his tumbler of bourbon to his lips. He gives me a wink, the gold band on his finger reflecting the overhead light. We're in the same club we came to for my twenty-eighth birthday when Logan and I were nothing more than friends. The first time we kissed, the first night we ever spent together, the night that our hearts decided to love each other and no one else.

"Happy Dirty Thirty!" Amy squeals, pulling me from my thoughts. Clinking her glass against mine, she kisses me square on the mouth.

"Hey now!" Logan protests with a smile, arms opened wide.

"I had her first you know." She says, placing one manicured hand against her hip, "You're lucky I let her marry you."

"Like you had any say." He teases, pulling away from the bar as people slap sloppy kisses against my cheek.

"It's true. Plus, don't forget you have me to thank for you guys meeting each other in the first place. I was the one who dragged her to that bar. And I was the one who got you guys back together."

"Hey!" This time it's Joanna protesting, taking the same offensive pose her brother just held. "I was the one who told her where he was, and I was the one who got Caleb to pick her up. If anyone deserves thanks, it's me."

Playfully rolling my eyes, I drape my arms loosely around Logan's neck, careful not to spill my drink on him. "Happy Birthday, Duck."

I smile broadly, pulling his mouth to mine.

His kiss promises me years of happiness and love. It promises a happily ever after with the man of my dreams.

I have him; I have everything, and I know it.

THE ART OF DATING

My name is Devina Marshal, and I fell in love with the man who taught me the art of dating.

...and the art of fucking like wild animals.

"What the hell?" I stare at the computer screen before twisting in my chair, jumping when I see Logan leaning against my office door in nothing but a pair of boxers, phone in hand. "What are you doing?"

"Adding." He nods to my screen, "You're still unbearably boring."

Shoving his ribs, I laugh, "Shut up, go write your own book."

"I can't. My favorite story's already been told." He says, claiming my mouse.

I watch him scroll through my novel, stopping when he gets to the morning after my twenty-eighth birthday, "Here we go."

Reading over the words, I notice they aren't mine. "You added your perspective?" I gawk at him.

Nodding, he kisses my cheek, "Now you know." He whispers.

"Know what?" My voice turns husky as his hand slides up my bare thigh, his face painfully close to mine.

"That I loved you first."

PLAYLIST

Let me love you - ATC, Alex Goot, & KHS
Cover
Dusk til Dawn - Zayn Ft. Sia
Come back home – Callum Scott
Eavesdrop - Civil Wars

Edited to-
Ruelle – On the other side
Ruelle- Monsters

ACKNOWLEDGEMENTS

To my amazing sister, Nae Nae,
For your endless encouragement and willingness to talk with me through the story and allowing me to freak out when I thought I'd never make it to the deadline, and having faith that I would all along. Love you cuntface.

My incredible family, for their support, encouragement, and understanding when I've needed to cancel plans to finish these books.

To my amazing bestie; Sam 'BamBam, the mad Bammer Jammer' Knowlton, for dropping what you were doing and helping me edit this on a dimes notice. Your love, encouragement, and never ending support helped make this book a thing. You're the shit. I love you.

My amazing BETA readers; Jenn, Sam, V, Paige, Janelle, and Yericka. ♥ Without you my sentences would still be missing every other word, my tenses would swap every other sentence, and I wouldn't have had the pure joy of rage comments through the entire story.

My PA, Samantha Theodore Knowlton, for taking the wheel when I was ready to start throwing stuff. You were the first to read The Art of Dating and give me feedback while helping me promote. You're the best! Thank you!

My PR, Mel Teo at Booksmacked, for being the massive book whore that you are. Thank you for your assistance and encouragement. Without you, the cover would still suck, and i wouldn't have had the courage to go through with this book.

Aimee Noalane, thank you, Mama, for all that do. You've repeatedly pulled my ass out of the fire with knowledge, wisdom, and endless encouragement. You will never know just how much you've helped me. ♥ Thank you. P.S #DamianIsMINE
You can find her series, No Regrets at; goo.gl/iJaxmg

Meagan Brandy for keeping me sane when I bit off WAY more than I could chew. You helped me feel less chaotic and panicked about deadlines, and it's nice to know we're in the same boat with expectations and new author jitters.
You can find Meagan's book, Fumbled Hearts, here: goo.gl/K4Wrf7

Last but not least; my reader's group. These women are so unbelievably supportive. You're excitement, encouragement, and love not only got me into the predicament of cutting this book ENTIRELY too close to the deadline, but it gave me the courage and the kick in my pants to get it done. You are all so patient and supportive; I'll forever be grateful. ♥

MEET THE AUTHOR

My name is not actually Ellie Messe; I have a pseudonym so that I can feel like the Batman of the author world. I write solely for my sister, whose name shall not be mentioned to protect her lesbian identity. I'm a fun loving book dragon who has the ability to make sailors blush with colorful language and obscene gestures. I love reading, mostly young adult and new age. I'm a part of a BANGerangin' book club that is guaranteed to be better than yours. I like to spend my days wondering around department stores while reading erotica out loud, scaring the piss out of people, and playing "The floor is lava." (Adulting is lame.)

Stay connected on Social Media:
-Instagram for teasers; @EllieMesseAuthor
-Let's be friends on Facebook; goo.gl/1W5mYj
-My reader's group for exclusive excerpts, first looks, and sneak peeks; goo.gl/wLa2q9
Other books: goo.gl/9JfKX1

THE ART OF DATING

OTHER BOOKS BY ELLIE MESSE:

BROKEN

(602 pages, Angst Romance)

Mama didn't come home.
Daddy liked to hit.
Brothers followed suit.

So I ran.

I ran from that life.
I ran from myself.
I ran into him.

I have no experience with the game board we're playing on, and that makes this a lethal game. One wrong move and my heart could land in the fire he's created inside me. Worse, it could lead my past to his doorstep and it won't just be my blood that taints this floor.

I should run. I need to run.

My father is the devil in a flesh suit, he won't be happy until he paints this town red for my betrayal.

I should run. I need to run.

Because despite my feelings for Parker Hayes, the devil is coming and he wants what's his.

Link:

https://www.amazon.com/Broken-Ellie-Messe-ebook/dp/B078JZFTXC/ref=sr_1_7?ie=UTF8&qid=1536055178&sr=8-7&keywords=broken